Bye Bye Bully

REVISED

Isabel M. Peña

ISBN: 978-1-64516-517-0   (Paperback Edition)
ISBN: 978-1-64516-516-3   (Hardcover Edition)
ISBN: 978-1-64516-518-7   (E-book Edition)

Some characters and events in this book are fictitious. Any similarity to real persons, living or dead, is coincidental and not intended by the author.

Book Ordering Information

Phone Number: 347-901-4929 or 347-901-4920
Email: info@globalsummithouse.com
Global Summit House
www.globalsummithouse.com

Printed in the United States of America

CONTENTS

Dedicated to my sons Daniel and Marcos Andujar.
They are the reason why I strive to become a
better person every day.

INTRODUCTION

"If men could only know each other,
they would neither idolize nor hate."

-Elbert Hubbard

*F*unny how we can change the way we view life when we learn to embrace it for what it is. Just as odd is how we allow fear to change who we really are. Since birth, we are given labels that we bear for the most part of our lives.

In the case of Mildred Riley, because she was abandoned by her mother when she was six, she was considered to be a child of a broken home. As a result, Mildred began to feel the weight of those labels. She found herself living in darkness and fear. Consequently, she grew angry and felt that life had cheated her out of what she deemed "normal." Hoping to gain the control and order that she so desperately needed, Mildred became a bully.

When Amanda Muse started her new school in a small town in Colorado, she immediately became a target for Mildred. Amanda was cute, sociable and part of a typical nuclear family which society would consider honorable and appropriate for a girl her age. Naturally, this engendered envy within Mildred, even though Amanda's home was not as perfect as it seemed. Being aware of this along with having a kind-hearted nature, Amanda was able to see past the labels and appreciate Mildred for who she really was.

When a freak accident led Mildred into Amanda's home, she was exposed to light, structure, responsibilities, and (most importantly) love. The accident gave Mildred an opportunity to reevaluate her life and know that even the most revered families are not entirely perfect. In turn, Amanda learned that bullies are many times, victims themselves. It was through their love and acceptance for each other that they were able to change for the better.

Hopefully, this story of two girls who initially couldn't bear the sight of each other but then became best friends can inspire today's youth to live by love and acceptance and to realize that we are not so different after all.

"He who strikes terror in others is himself continually in fear."

- Claudius Claudianus

CHAPTER 1

∙∙∙

Dreaded Signs

*B*ig things do come in small packages. One of these things is autumn. If only it could be autumn all year. The cool weather, the colors of the trees, and even what people wear is always nicer in the fall. It's football season. There's pumpkin flavored everything. Bonfires and s'mores are popular and so much fun. There's also that tingly feeling in your gut that comes from knowing that the holidays are just around the corner. It truly is spectacular!

There are back-to-school signs in department stores everywhere when fall is approaching. Some people will cringe at the sight of them while others get a taste of heaven. If you are a parent, then this is the sign that you have been waiting for all summer. For the kids, it's like opening the gates of hell. Well, for most kids anyway.

Mildred Riley was the one kid that didn't feel threatened by these signs. In fact, she couldn't wait for school to start. She looked forward to anything that kept her away from home. At Lakewood Junior High, she was the queen bee. Everyone else saw her as a big bully, but she didn't see herself that way. She just felt that she had the right to boss everyone around. After all, she was bigger than everybody else.

Mildred had spent five years bullying other kids. She had always been a big, strong girl, so it was pretty easy for her to be in charge of all the other kids. Mildred was really big for a kid her age and other kids were always afraid to stand up to her. Mildred had red hair, had freckles all over her body, and was a bit on the heavy side. She was not bad looking though.

Mildred lived in the Lakewood Terrace Apartments which was a residential area for low-income families. She lived there with only her dad, Joe Riley, because her mother had left them when Mildred was only six years old.

This was very hard for both Mildred and Joe. Joe worked long hours as a truck driver and many times had to leave Mildred with their elderly next-door neighbor, Alice, who would watch over Mildred while he was out working. As Mildred got older, Joe became more comfortable with leaving Mildred home alone. This meant that little Mildred had no choice but to grow up quickly.

The way that Joe dealt with his hard and stressful life was by drinking. He drank so much that he gradually developed a drinking problem. Incredibly, it didn't affect his work much, but Mildred never knew what to expect when her dad came home. This was why Mildred liked being in school. Not only was school an escape from her unstable reality, but it was also the only place where she felt safe and like she had some control over her life.

Mildred did not have many friends. Everybody was mostly afraid of her. She did, however, have one 'friend' in school and her name was Liz Lombardi. Liz waited on Mildred hand and foot. Liz, unlike Mildred, came from a wealthy Italian family. She was an only child and was very spoiled. In her parents' eyes, Liz could do no wrong. They could never imagine that Liz would associate herself with someone like Mildred Riley. They felt that Mildred was beneath their daughter. In spite of Liz's parents' illusions, this odd pair hung out most of the time that they were in school.

Liz was average sized, yet nobody dared to confront her either because she always had her bodyguard, Mildred, with her. Liz was not aggressive, but she always wanted to be on Mildred's good side so she went along with everything that Mildred did.

Most of the time, Mildred was just mean to everybody. There was one time, however, where Mildred did show some signs of humanity. There was another bully named Thomas Cook who was picking on a nerdy kid named Luis Alfonso. Thomas had urinated in an empty spray bottle and then he let the urine sit for three days. He then took the spray bottle and sprayed the fermented pee on Luis. Poor Luis spent the entire school day smelling like a gas station bathroom.

In an incredible twist, Mildred stood up to Thomas and proceeded to beat the crap out of him. Mildred was suspended for three days, but Thomas was actually expelled from school. Nobody was sure if Mildred felt sorry for Luis or if she just wanted to send the message that she was the only one who was to run the show at Lakewood Junior High. Whatever the case was, Luis was never picked on again, not by Thomas, not by Mildred, nor by anybody else. At least some good came out of it.

To be fair, Mildred wasn't always a bully. In fact, she was a very happy and loving little girl; or at least she was before her mother abandoned her and her dad.

Some say that her mother, Jennifer, was bipolar or suffered from major depression.

Others believed that she was going through a midlife crisis. But Mildred's dad knew that Jennifer had gone off with some younger guy and wanted to start all over from scratch.

This turn took a toll on Joe. He began to close himself off in his own little world.

When he would come home, he would sit on his couch and wait for seven-year-old Mildred to prepare him something to eat. Afterward, he'd turn the television on and booze his life away.

He never spoke to Mildred about her mother or much else for that matter. Mildred was just expected to care for her drunken dad. On a good day, Joe would pass out on the couch and Mildred would remove his shoes and socks, bring him a blanket and go lock herself up in her room. Her room was the only place in her home where she actually felt some peace.

Her room was full of her dolls. She loved being there just to get away from her father's nasty smell of feet and alcohol with the smallest hint of Right Guard deodorant. Mildred liked to play with her dollies, as she called them, by fantasizing that they had a picture-perfect family life. Toward the middle of the charade, the dolls always ended up in a horrific fight with each other. In the end, one of them would always end up being badly injured or killed.

On the other hand, there was Amanda Muse. Amanda was the tiniest and cutest girl you had ever met. Amanda was biracial. Her father, Eric Muse Sr., was African American and her mother, Victoria Muse, was white. Amanda had dark-brown curly hair, beautiful olive skin, and hazel eyes. Because she was small and thin, her peers (if they noticed her at all) considered her to be the perfect target for just about anything. She could easily be a victim of bullying or someone to carry out odd favors for everyone else. But despite appearances, Amanda was not a pushover. She was passive but very friendly, kind, and smart.

If you were to put Mildred and Amanda together, they'd look like the lion and the mouse. They were both starting the eighth grade, but Mildred looked as if she was starting her junior year in high school while Amanda looked like she was starting the third grade.

This year would be Amanda's first year in Lakewood Junior High. Her family moved from New York City to Colorado in hopes of finding a more family-oriented place. Amanda had an older brother named Eric Jr. who was sixteen and mildly autistic. Everyone called him Junior. Her parents felt that the stress level in the city kept them from dedicating quality time to the kids, especially Junior. They figured that once they were in Colorado, they would be able to spend more quality time with each other and enjoy their life.

For most people, the Muses seemed to be the perfect American family. Be that as it may, almost three years prior, Vicky found out that Eric had been having an affair with an Asian lady who was working in the same company as he was. There were even rumors that he had fathered a son with this other woman. There was a big falling out that year for the Muses. In the end, they decided to 'work things out' and move to another state to give themselves the opportunity to start fresh.

Even though Amanda had both of her parents and they appeared to be the 'perfect' family, her house was not exactly the Little House on the Prairie. Amanda had her share of drama and responsibilities at home as well. Having an autistic teenager in the home is not exactly a walk in the park. At times, her parents became overwhelmed with work, maintaining the household, taking care of one kid, and taking special care of their special kid.

Amanda had just turned thirteen but often found herself assisting her brother many times when it became too much for Vicky to handle. It was a good thing that Vicky worked from home. Nevertheless, after a long day's work, her mother had to prepare dinner and Amanda had to help out.

Junior liked to spin everything in the house. Lids, CDs, cups, you name it—he made it spin. Vicky's sister, Ivette, had given him some tops to spin, but for some reason, he just liked to spin random objects in the house. Junior was only mildly autistic, so he was capable of doing a lot of things that other kids his age did. He was also very good at math. In fact, he was a math genius. Junior did not attend a regular high school like other kids. Instead, he had a private tutor who would come to his house to teach him during the day.

With all of the drama that went on between the Muses three years prior, there was an inevitable tension in their home. Even though they came to Colorado to start fresh, sometimes those old demons crept up on them. They did try though.

For the most part, they were able to work out their differences. The point is that even though Amanda's family was together, they weren't perfect either. Gosh, is anybody's?

CHAPTER 2

· ·

Welcome to Lakewood Junior High!

*F*inally, August 29th rolled around. It was much anticipated for some and much dreaded for others because it was the first day of school. Amanda had all of her brand new back-to-school outfits, backpack, and supplies. Mildred, on the other hand, had all of her old clothes and supplies from two years before. Regardless, she was delighted to start the new school year. It seemed like summer would never end. When you're involved in the whole summer-fun shebang, then summer can go fairly quickly. For someone like Mildred though, who only stayed home during the summer, it can drag on forever.

Amanda was a ball of nerves. She had no idea how the kids in Colorado were. All she knew was that, for starters, she looked different. Most of the kids in Lakewood were as white as they come. She had never seen so many white kids together at one time in her life. Even though she was half white, she did not look it unless you met her mother.

A week before school started, Amanda had registered for school and was assigned a locker buddy named Lucinda Johnson. Like Amanda, Lucinda was not the type of kid that most people would take much notice of. She was about Amanda's height and very friendly. She was known for her colorful and slightly salty language. Other than that, she was just another girl in school.

Last December, that changed for Lucinda. During class, Lucinda sneezed and accidentally farted at the same time. Kids never let that kind of stuff go. She never heard the end of it. For Lucinda, it was pure horror. For others, it was sheer magic. Her only hope was that after the Christmas break the kids would forget all about the incident. Instead, they came back with vengeance. She was given the name 'Gassy Lucy' for the rest of the school year. Man, what a way to get noticed!

As Amanda approached her locker on that first day of school, Lucinda was right there waiting for her.

"Hi, you must be Amanda. I'm Lucinda, your locker buddy," said Lucinda with a big ol' smile.

"Yes, hi, nice to meet you, Lucinda," said Amanda with her cute, little, shy face.

"Just so you know, I took the top shelf, hope you don't mind. If you do, I'll take the bottom one. I really don't care."

"No, that's okay. The bottom shelf is fine with me. I'm not that tall anyway," replied Amanda.

As they both looked at their schedules, they said simultaneously, "So, what's your first period?"

They chuckled. Lucinda, out of nowhere, punched Amanda on the arm and shouted, "Punch buggy!"

Man, did Amanda hate that! She hoped that Lucinda was not one of those annoying friends that just hangs around you all the time and make you feel as if you can't hang out with anybody else. She also hoped that she wasn't the kind that makes other kids not want to hang out with you.

"I have biology first period," said Lucinda.

"Um, me too."

"Great! We can go together."

Both Amanda and Lucinda walked over to their biology classroom. When they walked in, they noticed that Mildred and her sidekick, Liz Lombardi, had it too. Mildred and Liz were new to Amanda, but not to Lucinda. Lucinda knew very well of Mildred's reputation as a bully and Liz's 'cheerleading' abilities.

The minute Amanda and Lucinda entered the classroom, Mildred blurted out, "Hey, Gassy Lucy, got a new friend?"

As they walked toward their chairs, Lucinda whispered to Amanda, "Just ignore her. That girl has some serious issues."

"Hey, Gassy Lucy, did you warn your new friend to maintain a respectable distance if it looks like you're going to sneeze?"

"That's enough Mildred!" said Mr. Erickson, the biology teacher, as he walked into the classroom.

Amanda looked at Lucinda and said, "Why does she call you Gassy Lucy?"

"Nothing, just ignore her okay. I told you she has issues."

"Everyone have a seat. Take out your notebook and a pen. We are going to take some notes on what you are expected to do in this class and what you will need for supplies," said Mr. Erickson.

Immediately, Liz whispered to Mildred, "The new girl is going to need some tissues and a bomb shelter."

Then Mildred added, "Yeah, and a can of Lysol."

"Mildred Riley, not in my class!" He took a breath before continuing. "Well class, it looks like we have a new student this year. Miss Amanda Muse, will you please stand up and tell us a little bit about yourself?"

This was very embarrassing for Amanda.

Amanda stood up hesitantly, and in a shaky, low voice said, "Hi, my name is Amanda Muse and I was born in New York City. I have an older brother, and I live with my mom and my dad."

At that very moment, Mildred felt a knot in the pit of her stomach. She only saw that Amanda's family seemed like a perfect family, and she hated Amanda for that. She loathed anybody who was privileged enough to not come from a broken home. The only reason Mildred tolerated Liz was because she knew that even though Liz lived with both of her parents, they were too busy to pay attention to Liz. Liz's parents spoiled her and gave Liz everything she wanted because they wanted to make up for not spending real quality time with her.

"Very well, Amanda. Welcome to Lakewood. Have a seat. Okay class, enough chatting. It's time for some biology."

By the time biology class was over, Amanda was feeling a little ill at ease. She could already tell that Mildred and Liz were bullies. To make matters worse, her tag-along friend, Lucinda, was one of Mildred's targets. Naturally, this would make Amanda a target by association. Amanda would not see Lucinda for the rest of the school day.

Math was Amanda's next period. This was also Mildred's next period. Mrs. Clancy was their math teacher. Mrs. Clancy was an Irish immigrant who arrived in Boston with her husband fourteen years ago. Shortly after their arrival, her husband was murdered by some thugs who waited for him to get out of work, to bang his head several times with a hammer before robbing him. He made it to the emergency room, but died two hours later. Mrs. Clancy never remarried. Instead, she decided to pick up and move west. She wound up in Colorado. When she got there, she went back to school and became a math teacher.

The minute Amanda walked in, she noticed that Mildred was already starting trouble. Mildred shoved a boy named Daniel Phillips out of his chair and threw his books on the floor.

"You're in my seat, twerp!" said Mildred.

"Mildred Riley!" yelled Mrs. Clancy from the back of the room.

"It's okay, Mrs. Clancy, I'll sit closer to the window," said Daniel.

He went to sit on a chair that was right next to Amanda.

She looked at him and said, "She's so mean!"

"I know," said Daniel, "I don't care though. If sitting on that chair makes her happy, then so be it. I'm Daniel, by the way. What's your name?"

"Amanda."

"Nice to meet you Amanda, you're going to love math. It's my favorite subject!"

Amanda had never met anybody who loved math except for Junior, her brother. But this was Daniel for you. He had always been very mature for his age, honest, and an easygoing guy. He was also kind of cute. Although he had many male friends, Daniel preferred to hang out with the girls. It was difficult for Daniel to relate to most guys. He was sensitive and not quite the athlete. He could relate more to girls because he felt that girls were at least open to talking about more meaningful things.

"I doubt it," said Amanda, "I'm not very good at math, but my brother, Junior, is like a genius in math. Seriously, he's like a math alien or something."

Daniel chuckled. "That's good though. You have me to help you out here in class and your bro can help you out at home."

"Yeah, I guess so."

As boring math went on, Amanda was counting the seconds until the end of the day. First days of anything always seem to go on much longer than any other day. The only highlight so far for Amanda was Daniel. The more she stared at him, the more she found things that were cute about him. He had dark brown hair, green eyes, the cutest little dimples, and he dressed very nice. Normally, guys who look this nice could care less about schoolwork, but not Daniel. He was cute and smart!

The day went on and Amanda, Lucinda, and Daniel met up at lunchtime. There, Daniel introduced Amanda and Lucinda to another girl named Sky Martin.

Sky was very sweet and very loveable. She wasn't much of a talker, but definitely a great listener. Sky could easily fit in with any group, but she liked this one best.

After lunch, the rest of the day went normally. Amanda did not see Mildred or Liz in any other of her classes until her last class of the day, PE. Amanda loved PE because she was very athletic. She was tiny, but she could run, bend, and jump with the best of them. To her dismay, the only familiar faces in PE were Mildred and Liz.

It didn't take long for Mildred and Liz to notice Amanda.

As Amanda was putting her stuff in her locker, Mildred slammed the locker door shut and said, "Hey, Booger, where are your friends?"

"Booger?" replied Amanda.

"That's right, Booger. I assume you came out of Gassy Lucy's nose. Or were you part of something else? Maybe something that came out of her ass?"

"What? What are you talking about?" said Amanda surprised.

"That's right, snot! Hasn't Gassy Lucy told you how she got her name? It's because she can't sneeze like normal people do. She needs gas to escort out her sneeze."

"What?" said Amanda confused.

"That's right, pea brain! Lucy sneezed and farted at the same time in class."

"So, that's what *that's* all about! Still, that's no reason to make fun of somebody," said Amanda innocently.

"It is too a reason!" said Mildred. "We shouldn't have to put up with her germs and gas all at once!"

"Yeah, snot," added Liz, "She's just nasty all around."

Then that famous PE whistle sounded: PRRRIIING!

"Let's go, Lakewooders!" said Ms. Woo, the PE teacher, "We only have forty-five minutes to get your little hearts pumping and your blood circulating!"

Then Mildred looked straight at Amanda and said, "Watch your step, Booger."

Mildred and Liz walked away laughing.

While everyone was running laps, Amanda was catching up to Mildred. When she was close enough, Mildred stuck her foot out and tripped Amanda really bad.

Amanda fell to the ground. As she looked up, Mildred said, "Oops! Told you to watch your step."

Amanda wanted to cry but refused to do so. She refused to let Mildred win this one. Amanda had only known Mildred for a couple of hours, but she was already getting on Amanda's last nerve. Everybody could tell that Amanda was tearing up, including Ms. Woo.

When Ms. Woo asked Amanda if she was okay, Amanda simply replied, "Yeah, I'm okay. It was just an accident."

"Yeah!" shouted Liz out of nowhere. "I saw it myself! She tripped over Mildred's foot by accident."

"Are you sure, Amanda?" asked a concerned Ms. Woo.

"Yes, Miss, I'm sure."

"Very well class, let's keep moving!" said Ms. Woo.

After that incident, Mildred and Liz relaxed a little bit. They had gotten their bullying fix for the day. Besides, they figured that Amanda got the message. Mildred and Liz were setting the tone for that school year. Amanda understood it well.

When the day was finally over, Amanda decided that it wasn't that bad of a day after all, despite Mildred and Liz. Amanda felt that most of the kids were nice, and even the teachers were nice. She had Daniel, Lucinda, and Sky to look forward to the next day. Even though Amanda was a little scared, it was nice to know that she had the support of her new friends.

CHAPTER 3

···

A New Friend

O n the way home, Amanda decided to walk across Lakewood Park. This park was a beautiful park. There was a nice lake with ducks all around as well as trails that led to woody areas. It also had a small stage where people could perform plays or small concerts. People who frequented the park had their own little spots they hung out in.

Like everything else, Lakewood Park had its good things and its bad things. A lot of wannabe hippies hung out there, smoking and getting high. There was also a homeless population that camped out in the woody areas near the trails.

Many of the trails had huge rocks along them. If you walked along the trails, then you would need to watch out for falling rocks. There were signs all along the trails that read, 'Watch for Falling Rock.' However, most people would walk right past them even though there had been reports of rocks actually falling.

The park was definitely a longer walk to Amanda's house. Nonetheless, Amanda preferred to walk the extra distance because she had noticed that Mildred walked in the same direction to go home. Amanda figured that if she cut through the park, then she would avoid any extra trouble.

As Amanda was walking through the trails, she heard a dog barking in the distance. It was hard to tell where the bark was coming from at first, but as she walked, she could hear the bark getting louder and closer. She realized that it was coming from behind her. Her heart nearly came out of her chest as she turned around to see a huge Rottweiler coming toward her. Her first thought was, 'Cujo!'

You see, Amanda's parents seemed to be stuck in the 1980's. They listened to all of the 1980's music; they watched all of the 'Brat Pack' movies and all of the 1980's scary movies. Cujo, which was a movie about a mother and her son who were trapped in a car because a Saint Bernard with rabies was torturing them, was one of the movies they had on rotation. Even though Amanda was not allowed to watch these scary movies, her parents had spent enough time talking about them that Amanda was very familiar with them. Needless to say, Amanda was terrified of this dog.

Amanda knew not to run, even though she could have probably given this dog a run for its money. She was fast, and from the looks of it, the dog seemed old and not in the best of shape. She decided to grab a big rock from the ground in case she needed to defend herself with it.

As the dog drew closer to her, it began to slow down. Amanda could tell that the dog was out of shape or maybe even sick.

Then, out of nowhere, she heard, "Coco! Coco! What'cha doin', girlfriend? You come back here thith inthtant!"

It was a big, 6'2" man yelling for his dog. The man was dirty, feminine, and he had a slight speech impediment. It didn't take long before Amanda had determined that the man was one of the homeless people who camped out in the park. She wasn't sure if she should allow herself to be scared or not. She was in the middle of nowhere and out came this stranger and his big dog. She had every reason to be scared. The man approached her panting and completely out of breath.

Looking at his dog, he said, "Girlfriend, you are going to kill me one day!" Then he turned his attention to Amanda. "And you little lady, are you all right? Watcha doin' walkin' the trailth all by yourthelf anyway? Don't you know how dangerouth thith ith?"

A little shaken, Amanda replied, "Um, yes, sir. I'm on my way home from school. I thought this would be a nicer walk."

"Well, unleth you live here in the park, thith ith alwayth a longer way," said the stranger.

"I understand, sir," she replied.

"Well, you can call me Bo, and thith here ith my dog, Coco. Like me, she lookth big and thcary, but she'th harmleth. If you don't mind, we will be ethcorting you out of thethe trailth to make sure you make it home thafe today."

"Oh no, that's okay. You don't have to. I'm fine, really."

"Come on, kid, we're not going to hurt ya. If I wanted to hurt ya, thith here would be the betht plathe to do so. There'th no one around and you are in the middle of nowhere. Bethideth, and in cathe you haven't notithed, I'm very maternal. You've mutht have notithed. Can't you tell how I am practically a breatht?"

Chuckling, Amanda said, "I guess it's okay."

"Of courthe, it ith. We won't hurt you kid. I am jutht too out of shape to do you harm, and my girlfriend Coco, why, she'th jutht too old for her own good."

Amanda reluctantly agreed. As they started to walk, Bo said, "Zo tell me, little lady, what ith your name and why do you choothe a much longer and not zo thafe way to get home?"

"My name is Amanda, Amanda Muse. I don't know, I really thought it would be a nice walk and well…" She paused to consider what she was going to say. "…I just thought it would be nice that's all."

"A-hum. Are you sure that ith it?"

Looking toward the ground, Amanda said, "Well, I'm new in town and it was my first day of school today and already there's this big girl, a bully, who's starting to look for trouble. I feel a bit safe in school, but I was afraid of bumping into her after school. This is why I chose to cut through the park."

"I zee. Hmm. Bullying ith thomething I'm much too familiar with."

"Really? But you are such a big guy! How can a big guy like you be bullied?" said Amanda.

"Come on girl, look at me! What'th not to bully? Thometimeth bullying ith not a phythical thing. Thometimeth people jutht hate you for being you. Wanna know what my real name ith?"

"I thought it was Bo," Amanda said innocently.

"No girly girl, my name ith James, James Anderson," Bo said trying to sound 'normal.'

For some reason, Bo was able to pronounce his real name without his lisp coming out.

"So why do they call you Bo?"

Taking a deep breath followed by a big sigh, Bo said, "My Uncle Charlie thought it wath appropriate becauthe he zaid that I wath not completely a boy. Don't get me wrong, my Uncle Charlie ith the cooletht. He ith the only one who really loveth me for me, even if he thinkth that I am mithing the 'Y' chromothone that maketh a human being a male."

"I'm sure your parents love you too. Don't they? I mean, all parents love their children even if they don't know how to show it, don't they?"

"I really don't know about that kid. I gueth. The way I zee it, love should be unconditional. It shouldn't be thomething you feel toward people who are like you or who think the thame ath you."

"My mom says that sometimes parents love their kids so much that they fear for them. Maybe your parents fear that all the other people will harm you. Where are your parents anyway?"

"I gueth. My father died of a heart attack when I wath eighteen; he wath only forty-zix. Four yearth later, they found a cantherouth tumor in my mom'th brain that killed her."

"Sorry to hear that, Bo."

"It'th okay. I've moved on."

Amanda and Bo were so into their conversation that time flew by. Before they knew it, they had walked the trails and crossed the entire park.

When the streets and residential areas were in view, Amanda turned to Bo. "Well, thanks for walking me. It was really nice talking to you."

"Oh my! We crothed the park already? Well, little lady, if you dethide to croth over the park again tomorrow, you know where to find me. It wath really nithe talkin' to ya."

"Thanks again, Bo. I will see you soon."

With that, Amanda headed home. She felt happy and good as she went the rest of the way. The minute she walked into her house, Amanda could smell that something was not right. In one nostril she smelled delicious home cooking. In the other nostril, she smelled the unmistakable smell of poop. Her brother, Junior, had had a little accident. Apparently, he had almost made it to the bathroom, but as he pulled his pants down, he began to go. Some fell in and on the toilet, but some had fallen on the floor. Amanda's mother, Vicky, was already taking care of it.

"Oh Amanda, honey, I'm so glad you're home! What took you so long? If I wasn't picking up after your brother, I would've been on the phone with the police!"

"Sorry, Mom. I decided to cut through the park today."

"The park? Why the park? Amanda, I don't want you cutting through the park anymore. Do you hear me, young lady? Why would you cut through the park anyway?"

"I just thought it would be nice Mom, that's all. You don't have to worry. A really nice man named Bo and his dog Coco walked me so I wouldn't have to walk by myself."

"A nice man? A dog? You mean a stranger! Amanda, honey, you should know better! What are you doing talking to strangers?"

"I know Mom, I'm not dumb. Trust me, he is really nice."

"Where does this stranger live? Is he from this area?"

"Um, he's kinda homeless."

"What? A homeless stranger named 'Bum' with a flea-infested dog? Okay, I've heard enough. No more walking the park with 'Bum' or any other bums for that matter. I'm serious!"

"It's Bo, Mom, and he's not like that. He protected me and I felt safe around-"

"This is not open for discussion! It's final."

"Okay, Mom. So, what did you cook today?"

"I grilled some steaks. I was going to make mashed potatoes, but got caught up. You can put some garlic bread in the toaster oven and we can all have grilled steaks with garlic bread."

"Sounds good, Mom."

"Other than Mr. Bo and his dog, how was your first day of school? Met any friends?"

"Actually, Mom, it was pretty nice. I met a girl named Lucinda, another girl named Sky, and a boy named Daniel. They were all very nice. All the teachers were really nice too."

Amanda did not feel the need to mention Mildred. She did not want her mother to worry.

"Oh wonderful, honey! I'm glad you are enjoying your new school."

They continued on with the rest of their day. Amanda's dad came home a little late that night, but he managed to spend some quality time with his family. Eric was a real-estate agent and his conversations regarding work were not very interesting. He was well aware of it, so he just listened to everybody else's day instead of talking about his day. Both Vicky and Amanda vowed not to mention the park or Bo to Eric. Vicky trusted that Amanda would keep her promise not to cut through the park again.

CHAPTER 4

....

The Horror

As time went on, Amanda tried her best to get the hang of school. However, Mildred and Liz made it extremely difficult. They continued making their wisecracks here and there. They were always finding ways to bully her. They would do anything from taking Amanda's lunch money to shoving her head in a toilet bowl and demanding that she drink the toilet water.

On better days, Mildred made Amanda eat disgusting things like old chewing gum that had been stuck underneath a desk for who knows how long. Mildred never did anything in front of anybody. She always waited for Amanda to be alone. Amanda was too afraid of what Mildred would do to her if she said anything. Therefore, Amanda never reported the bullying to anyone. The only person she felt comfortable enough around to talk about it was Bo.

One time, Mildred found Amanda alone in the bathroom. She picked a fresh booger out of her nose and tried to force Amanda to eat it. Luckily, some girls came in to use the restroom. This was enough to make Mildred stop immediately. This bullying went on throughout the beginning of the school year. There were days that Amanda was so depressed that she didn't even want to go to school. Even on those bad days, though, she had great friends that helped and supported her any way that they could.

During school hours, Amanda felt safe to some degree. She knew that even if Mildred bullied her, Mildred could only go so far before getting into trouble. After school, however, was a totally different story. Amanda did not have the support of her friends or the presence of the teachers to make her feel safe. She was petrified of walking home by herself, so she completely disregarded the promise she made to her mother and continued to cut through the park to avoid Mildred.

Occasionally, she would bump into Bo. She'd talk to him for a bit to vent her feelings about the situation when it got to be too much. When it became October, the temperature went down dramatically. Amanda worried about how hungry and cold Bo and Coco must be out there. Whenever she could, Amanda would take him any leftover lunch that she had.

Despite all that was happening in her life, Amanda had made quite a name for herself in school. She was quite the athlete at Lakewood Junior High. Most kids would fight to have Amanda on their team. Amanda's rapport with others only infuriated Mildred even more. Her anger and envy toward Amanda grew and grew. Mildred could not bear to see how perfect Amanda's life was while her own seemed to get gloomier by the second.

Amanda was still hanging out with Lucinda, Daniel, and Sky. The group of four met every day for lunch. But for a whole week, Amanda had not been feeling like herself. She had not been sleeping very well and was feeling a bit cranky and emotional about everything. Even her friends started to notice that she was acting differently. They knew that she had enough going on.

On the thirteenth day of October, everyone was having lunch as usual. Amanda had been complaining of having a headache all morning and not feeling very well. Vicky had given Amanda some aspirin before going to school. It made her feel a little bit better, but she was still feeling a little down emotionally.

During lunchtime, Amanda sat between Daniel and Sky with Lucinda on the opposite side of the table. As luck would have it, Mildred and Liz were having their lunch at a table right behind them. Suddenly, Amanda felt a horrible sharp pain in her abdomen and she felt wet. As she put her head down in pain, she noticed that her chair was almost completely covered in blood. Time froze for a second or two.

Amanda had no idea what was going on. She had heard of girls getting their periods, but she did not know that it would happen to her like this. For a second, she thought that maybe she had been stabbed. She did not say a word, but she inhaled so deeply and abruptly that Daniel and Sky looked down in horror. Daniel and Sky both pushed their chairs back and away from Amanda.

Somewhat loudly, Sky exclaimed, "Amanda, you've got your period!"

Lucinda, who was sitting across the table, got up and said, "Really? Let me see!"

"Holy crap!" Daniel added.

Amanda didn't move. She didn't even know what she should do about this whole mess. As if it was not horrifying enough, Mildred and Liz turned around to see what was going on. Mildred was speechless. She was as affected, perhaps even more so, as Amanda by this gory sight of blood. At least Amanda had heard of periods before. Ironically, big, smartass Mildred had no idea what periods were!

Could you blame her though? Mildred did not have a mother figure and her troubled father was not about to sit down and have 'the talk' with her. Mildred didn't know what to think about this. She had never seen so much blood in her entire life.

Liz, on the other hand, was well aware of puberty. Her mother had 'the talk' with Liz when Liz was ten. Liz still did not have her period, but she knew she'd be getting it someday. Heck, she was even looking forward to it!

Liz thought very highly of herself and felt that she was too much of a lady to discuss such things. Despite all this, Liz's 'daintiness' went out the window when she saw the blood on Amanda's chair.

"Oh my god!" she yelled, "Amanda Muse got her period!"

Liz could not have said it any louder. Before you knew it, the entire cafeteria was aware of the 'menstrual situation.' Normally, girls don't get a large amount of blood the first time they get their periods. However, Amanda had taken some aspirin that morning. Aspirin, because it is a blood thinner, had made her bleed excessively. Amanda had more blood on that chair than what would be included in a vampire's stew. It really looked like a stabbing.

Scared and embarrassed out of her mind, Amanda said hysterically, "Oh my god, Sky! What should I do? If I get up, then everyone's going to see . . ."

"Just go, Mandy! Go to the school nurse right now! Everyone already knows anyway, just go!" Sky replied quickly.

Daniel got up and grabbed the bloody chair. "It's okay Mandy, I'll get someone to clean this up."

"I'll go with you," said Lucinda.

"Make way everybody!" screamed Liz. "Make way for Bloody Mandy!"

All this time, Mildred was at a loss for words. She had never seen so much blood in her life. She was very shaken by it and too embarrassed to ask what a period was. Mildred just didn't understand why Amanda looked like she was hemorrhaging.

By the time Lucinda and Amanda got to the nurse, Amanda was bawling her eyes out. Lucinda had to explain everything to the nurse. Of course, first-time period situations were no strange thing to this nurse.

"It's okay, Amanda. Everything's going to be just fine," said the nurse, "I am calling your home right now. Do you want someone to bring you a new set of clothes or would you rather-"

"No!" interrupted Amanda, "I want my mother to come pick me up! Please! Just ask her to come get me. I just want to go home!"

"Okay, Amanda. I'll ask your mother to come get you. Right now I want you to go to the restroom, clean yourself up as much as you can, and stick this pad on your underwear."

Vicky worked from home which made it easy for her to just pick up and leave whenever she needed to.

"Okay. Please tell her to hurry, please!" Amanda said shaking from all the emotions.

The nurse called Vicky and asked her to come pick up her daughter as soon as possible. Lucinda waited with Amanda. After a couple of minutes, Daniel and Sky showed up to check up on Amanda.

Sky said, "So, how are you doing?"

"I just want to go home, that's all," said Amanda, calming down and looking forward to leaving.

"By the way, I already took care of the chair," said Daniel. "They told me to look for a janitor, but I felt that a cleaning lady would be more appropriate being that she's a girl and everything."

"Thanks, Danny," said Amanda. "Thank you all. You are all good friends. I don't know what I would have done without you guys."

"No worries, girl," said Sky, "I'm sure we will all have our days. One day, me and Lucy will get our periods and be all embarrassed and freak out too."

They all chuckled a little.

"Yeah, I won't get my period, but I hear that I'll be getting unexpected erections for no apparent reason and they will happen when I least want them to," Daniel added.

They all started to laugh just as Vicky walked in.

"Hey, honey, are you okay? They called me and told me that you were hysterical. You *are* hysterical, aren't you?"

"Yes, Mom, I am or at least I was. My friends here were just cheering me up a little. I'm just glad you're finally here. By the way, these are my friends Lucinda, Daniel, and Sky."

"Nice to meet you guys. Thanks for standing by Amanda's side."

"It was no problem at all, Mrs. Muse," said Daniel in his mature and 'good-boy' voice.

"Yeah, it was no trouble at all," said Sky.

"She's had a rough day today, Mrs. Muse," added Lucida, "But we hope she feels better and that we can see her tomorrow."

"Of course you will," said Vicky, "Amanda is going to be just fine. Thank you all again for your support. You are all good friends. Let's go, Amanda honey. Your brother is home with the tutor."

"Okay guys, see ya," said Amanda.

All three responded at once. "Bye Mandy, hope you feel better."

On their way home, Vicky didn't say much except, "You know what this means, don't you?"

"What?"

"It means that you have to be careful when you play with the boys."

"Huh?" Amanda was completely lost.

"That's right, young lady. If you're not careful playing with the boys, then you can end up with a baby."

"Oh, that."

They had arrived at the house. The two got out of the car. Vicky continued. "Yes, that. Now go take a warm bath and I'll make you some chamomile tea."

"Tea? Tea for what? I'm not even sure if I like tea."

"Chamomile tea is great for when you get your period, honey. My mom always made me chamomile tea when I had my lady days. She told me that it was very good for cramps."

"Did it work?"

"It always made me feel a little better. Now go on, honey, go take that warm bath."

Amanda went to the bathroom and started to prepare for her bath. Not two minutes had passed after closing the bathroom door, when Amanda overheard Vicky speaking to her sister, Ivette, telling her the breaking news.

"Yup, a-hum, yep. I know! She's all grown up now. Yes! I had to pick her up from school and everything. Apparently, she had a little accident. Poor baby was having lunch and-"

"Mom!" Amanda screamed from the bathroom.

"What is it, dear?" Vicky's response was followed by a slightly quieter, "Hold on, Ivette."

"What are you doing?" Amanda asked. She was starting to freak out again.

"I'm preparing your tea, sweet pea."

"No, you're not, Mom! You're telling Auntie Ivette!"

"That's okay, sweetheart. I can make your tea and talk to my sister all at one time. I'm good like that," Vicky said with a teasing tone.

"Mom! Don't! Please!"

"Listen, Ivette, I'll talk to you later, okay? Amanda is having a little conniption fit. Okay, bye."

Vicky hung up the phone and yelled back to Amanda, "Okay, sweet pea, I'm all done now."

"Thank you!" Amanda sighed and continued to try and relax in her bath.

When Amanda was done, she came out of the bathroom. The house smelled of cinnamon, cloves, apples, and chamomile.

"Hey, Mom, that smells pretty good," she said. "Is that my tea? Mom?" But Vicky was nowhere in sight. Amanda couldn't even hear her.

Amanda began to look for her mother and eventually found Vicky in her bedroom whispering on the phone. "Yes, I know, she's a big girl now. It was a terrible way to begin her menstrual cycle but-"

"Mom! I do not believe you! "

"Don't worry, honey. It's just your dad. I *have* to tell your dad!"

"Whatever, Mom! Can I have my tea now?"

"Sure, hun."

Her mother hung up the phone and gave Amanda her tea. They both sat and enjoyed their tea together. They also had a meaningful woman-to-woman conversation about what was going on. Amanda did feel a whole lot better after the tea. She was trying to adjust to the idea that she was now a young lady. She also needed to get used to the huge pad that she had to wear for a whole week.

The following day, Amanda returned to school. She did not know how to feel about it. She wondered if everything was going to be back to normal or if she would be the talk of the school. For a while, Mildred and Liz were calm with their bullying and name calling. They had a tendency to switch their victims from time to time, but if they let go of this incident, it would be a miracle.

When Amanda arrived at school, she noticed all kinds of mixed reactions. Some kids were smiling and sympathetic, others walked passed her as if nothing ever happened, and others giggled and whispered to their friends. Amanda was not sure what to make of it, so she just kept moving.

When she got to her locker, she noticed a sticky note posted on her locker door. It read, 'Bloody Mandy's Locker. DON'T TOUCH!' Stunned, she removed it right away. She looked around to see if anybody had noticed before she started to get ready for art class.

Lucinda arrived just a few moments later. "Hey, Mandy, how are you feeling today?"

"I'm good, I guess. I just found this sticky note on our locker door." Amanda showed Lucinda the sticky note.

"That bitch!" Lucinda said angrily.

"Who?" asked Amanda.

"What do you mean 'who?' Mildred, that's who. Mildred or her little monkey, Liz. They must have put it there this morning. Come on, let's go to class and settle this." Lucinda was determined to seek justice.

"What do you mean, Lucinda? What are you going to do? This is really not a big deal."

"You don't understand, Mandy. This is now your name forever. Unless somebody stands up to them, they are never going to stop. It's not only us, they've been bullying everyone else around, too. It's gotta stop! I've had it! Enough is enough!"

"Just don't do anything stupid or you're the one who's going to get in trouble."

"I won't. Trust me, I won't."

When they entered the classroom, they noticed Mildred and Liz sitting quietly on their chairs with their hands folded like they were perfect little angels. Amanda went to her seat and noticed that there was another sticky note that read, 'BEWARE! Bloody Mandy's chair.' Lucinda had also noticed a jar of red paint on the counter with another sticky note that read, 'SAFE. NONTOXIC RED PAINT. NON-BLOODY MANDY BLOOD.'

There were only a couple of students in the classroom, but Lucinda did not care. Despite her height, she was willing to fight for this whether she won or lost.

She was fed up about all of the bullying and name calling. She was not going to stand for it any longer.

Lucinda walked up to both Mildred and Liz and said, "You did this, didn't you? You low life pieces of . . ."

Before she finished her sentence, Mildred got up. She was looking down at Lucinda when she said, "That's right, Farts R' Us! What'cha gonna do about it, huh?"

Lucinda was not ready to back down just yet. She could almost feel her blood boiling and was prepared to fight if she had to. Luckily, their art teacher, Ms. Rogers, walked in just in time.

"Ladies, is there a problem?" she said sternly.

Ms. Rogers, although very pleasant, was also very strict. She had to be. It was the only way kids would take her art class seriously. She was also the principal's sister, which helped ensure that kids did respect her.

Lucinda and Mildred's eyes were locked in with each other and they seemed to communicate silently in that moment. Mildred's eyes were saying, "You better shut up and not say anything, twerp." Lucinda's eyes were telling Mildred, "You're going down, bitch!"

Without looking away from Mildred, Lucinda said, "Actually, Ms. Rogers, there *is* a problem."

"Excuse me?" Ms. Rogers sounded surprised.

Amanda discreetly and quietly handed Lucinda all of the sticky notes that she had seen that day.

Turning toward Ms. Rogers, Lucinda said, "This here is the problem, Ms. Rogers. These two low life bullies are writing these notes about Amanda and sticking them everywhere. I'm not sure if you know, but Mandy had a girl accident yesterday in the cafeteria, and these two are not letting it go."

"Let me see those notes, Lucinda," said Ms. Rogers.

"That wasn't us!" said Liz in a desperate attempt to save herself.

Unlike Mildred, Liz would get into trouble at home if she misbehaved. Liz's parents saw her as a perfect little angel and expected her to act like one at all times. They had no idea that their daughter had been playing the devil's advocate in school.

"Did you do this Mildred?" asked Ms. Rogers.

"No, ma'am. I did not."

"That's a lie, Ms. Rogers! She told me that she did it herself!" said Lucinda.

Ms. Rogers looked around at the classroom. "Class, do you know who did this?"

Immediately, the few kids that were there, some also victims of Mildred and Liz's bullying, joined in with Lucinda and said unanimously, "Yes, Ms. Rogers, they did it."

"You guys are so dead!" said Mildred angrily and pointing at the class.

"Okay, tough girls, let's go to the principal's office," said Ms. Rogers.

Ms. Rogers, Mildred, Liz, and the sticky notes headed off to the principal's office. The other kids in the classroom were very proud of Lucinda for standing up to them. They even offered their support if she ever needed it. The group suddenly realized something. As long as they were a group, then they were a bit safer.

When the rest of the class came in, they were all talking about what happened. Everyone was happy that they fought back. Later on, they found out that Mildred was suspended for three days because she had refused to apologize. She was also given a warning that she was not to bully anyone anymore. If she did bully anyone, then she'd be expelled from school.

Since this was the first time Liz had gotten into trouble, she was let go with a warning. Ms. Rogers made her write a two-page essay as punishment, though. The first page was to be about puberty and the second page about bullying. Liz was able to return to class with the condition that she apologized to Amanda, which she did. Mildred was asked to pick up her things and go home.

Some kids, after getting into trouble, may see suspension as vacation time, but this was not the case for Mildred. Even though she was not going to get into trouble with her father, she just hated being home. Being home was punishment enough for Mildred.

Amanda and Lucinda were not sure what was going to happen when Mildred returned to school. They wondered if she would be so angry that she would retaliate. Maybe this time she had learned her lesson. Who knew? Whatever the case may be, they figured they'd cross that bridge when they get there. It was Friday, and they intended to enjoy it without Mildred in school. Mildred was set to return on the following Thursday. That gave them almost an entire week of peace to enjoy.

CHAPTER 5

· ·

A Blast from the Past

*I*t was safe to say that the Muse family was a very typical one. They had their issues, but who doesn't? Vicky was a typical mom who took care of most of the household. Eric, Amanda's dad, was the breadwinner. He worked for a real-estate company and was very successful at his job. Even when he was feeling exhausted from a long day's work, he managed to spend time with his family. He didn't talk much, but he was a very good listener. He always took the time to ask everybody at home about their day.

For a week or so, the family had noticed that Eric was a bit distant, to say the least. He would get home, shower, eat, and go straight to his room. When anyone spoke to him, he seemed lost in his own world and would respond with noises instead of actual words. Everyone assumed that he was just tired from work, but Vicky started to get suspicious. Her old demons began to torment her again because she was beginning to feel as if history was repeating itself. She started to suspect that Eric was having an affair.

Naturally, Vicky faked it in front of the kids, but there was no fooling her. There's an old saying, 'A woman's intuition is more reliable than a man's certainty.' Vicky knew that there was something going on with her husband, and she was determined to get to the bottom of it.

At the dinner table, there was a tense, awkwardness that was making everyone feel uneasy. The feeling was so intense that everyone, except Junior, didn't touch most of their food. Amanda couldn't bear the tension. She excused herself and headed up to her room to work on homework or anything that could get her away from the dinner table.

When everybody was done with dinner, Vicky began picking up as usual. Eric volunteered to help.

"Babe, do you need me to help you with anything else? Do you need help in the kitchen?" he said after they had cleaned up most of the table.

The last time Eric offered to help out in the kitchen was the day that Vicky found out that he had been cheating on her with his co-worker, Susan Eng. Susan was a bright, Chinese lady who was the head of the marketing department in a prestigious advertising company. Eric was her assistant and they spent a lot of time with each other. Eventually, they ended up getting romantically involved. They both knew that it was wrong, but both of them felt unfulfilled in their personal lives at the time.

Eric and Susan were very discreet because of Eric's marriage, and Susan's very traditional and strict Chinese family. Dating a man who was not Chinese was not an option for Susan. If her family had found out that she was dating any man who was not Chinese, then it would have resulted in shame, dishonor, and disinheritance from her family.

One day, while Vicky was emptying out her husband's jacket to wash it, she found a receipt for a dozen white roses. Vicky never got these roses. When she confronted Eric about it, he came clean right away and told her the truth. He told her that he indeed had been having an affair and that it had been going on for two whole years. He explained to Vicky that the pressures of family life and work had pushed him into having this affair. He also told her that he was never in love with Susan. He went on telling Vicky how his family meant everything to him and that he could never imagine his life without them. Eric made a mistake by having this affair, but he was very devoted to his family and loved them very much.

Eventually, Vicky decided to give Eric a second chance, and that's how they ended up moving to Colorado.

And so there they were, Eric and Vicky in the kitchen, with tension so thick in the air that you could have cut it with a knife. Vicky couldn't take it anymore. Since Amanda was locked up in her room and Junior was spinning bowls somewhere, she took that opportunity to speak out.

Just as she opened her mouth to say something, Eric said, "Hey babe, do you want me to set these dishes in the dishwasher?"

"Oh cut the crap, Eric!" she said, throwing the rag in the sink.

"You need to tell me what the hell is going on with you! For the past week, you've been acting strange, and I know you, Mr. Muse. Now you want to help me out in the kitchen? Since when do you help me out in the kitchen?"

Exhaling a big sigh, Eric said those dreaded four words that nobody wants to hear, "Babe, we need to talk."

"Eric, what is it?" Vicky said, already smelling a rat.

"Come on, babe. Let's go upstairs to talk about it," he said. His voice was soft and calm, as if he was trying to comfort his wife.

They went upstairs to their bedroom and when they got there, Eric slowly closed the bedroom door behind him.

Vicky initiated the conversation by saying, "Eric, what's going on? You're really scaring me right now."

"I know, babe, and I'm so sorry. The first thing that I want to tell you is that I'm not having an affair. I know that that's what you are thinking."

"What can be worse than that, Eric? The way that you've been acting lately, tells me that it has to be something serious. Are you ill? Did you lose your job? For the love of God, Eric, tell me what is going on!"

"I'm not ill and I haven't lost my job, but it is serious. Remember Susan?"

"Of course. How can I forget? What about Susan?"

"Well, she's moving back to China. Her parents have arranged for her to get married to a man they have chosen for her."

"And?" Vicky paused, but then she grew more confused. "Wait. How do you know this? Have you been talking to her?"

"No, I promise. When I told you it was over, I meant it. I really did."

"So how do you know this?"

"She emailed me and told me."

"Okay, go on."

Eric sighed again. "Victoria, Susan and I have a son."

"What? A son? Eric, how could you? How could you do this to us?"

"Babe…"

"Don't call me babe!"

"Victoria, I didn't know because she never told me!"

"So why is she telling you now?"

"She can't move to China and get married if she has a son out of wedlock. She told me that if I didn't claim custody of my son, then she would give him up for adoption. I don't want my son to be given up for adoption, Vicky. He's my son! I just can't allow that to happen."

Ten seconds slowly ticked by before Victoria opened her mouth. With a low tone and a pang of hurt in her voice, she said, "I need to go out for a walk."

With a shattered heart, Vicky walked downstairs. Amanda, who was in her room, could still feel the tension in the house. When she heard her mother going down the stairs, she came out and followed her.

As Vicky was putting on her coat, Amanda asked, "Mom, where are you going?"

"Out for a walk, sweet pea."

"Anywhere in particular?"

"Nope. Just going out for a walk."

Being that the family had barely touched their dinner, there was a lot of leftovers. Amanda immediately thought of Bo and how he could probably use some food.

"Can I go with you, Mom?" said Amanda, "I would like to go to the park and give Bo and his dog all of the leftover food instead of throwing it out. I want you to meet him, too. He must be cold and hungry right now. Oh please, Mom, please!?"

Vicky figured that it would just be easier to comply than to resist and have to explain to her daughter why she didn't want to walk with her and do some good. Vicky agreed to go take some food to Bo.

"You're going to really like Bo, Mom, I just know it!" Amanda was ecstatic. Vicky, on the other hand, seemed lost, deep in her own thoughts.

"I'm sure, hun, if you say so."

"And his dog, Coco, too, Mom. She's really cool! She looks a little bit like Cujo, only nicer."

"That's nice, honey," said Vicky as they set out for the park.

They got to the park to find that it looked dark and eerie. Vicky was feeling uneasy about the situation, but because she had so much on her mind, she didn't mind it as much as she normally would have. As they were entering the wooded area, they began to see scattered tents and campfires. Amanda was not sure if she'd find Bo, but she was very hopeful. Suddenly, she heard barking close by. Amanda was sure that it was Coco.

She yelled, "Coco! Coco, is that you? Bo?"

"Oh, honey, are you sure?" said Vicky, her protectiveness and concern started to kick in.

Then they heard, "Hello? Who'th lookin'?"

Amanda immediately recognized that voice. It was an unmistakable voice. She became very excited and told her mother, "It's him, Mom, it's him! It's Bo, come on!"

She grabbed Vicky's hand and started to walk quickly in the direction that they had heard his voice from.

As they drew near, Amanda said, "Bo, it's me, Amanda."

"Hey, little lady, what'th up? It'th been a while. How have you been? And who'th thith lovely lady wit'cha?"

"Hi, Bo. I am Vicky. I'm Amanda's mother. It is nice to finally meet you, Bo.

Amanda has told me nothing but good things about you."

"Nithe to meet you, too. What bringth you over to the park at thith time?"

Amanda, with her cute little face all lit up said, "We thought you and Coco would like some food."

Bo glowed with excitement and said, "The good Lord never zeithes to amathe me! Thank you zo much, dear. Coco and I are sure going to enjoy thith! And thank you, ma-am."

Vicky had not said much the whole way, but found it incredible that this man, who had nothing to his name but a sick old dog, had such a grateful and cheerful disposition. She thought of how she had a warm home, a beautiful family, and three hearty meals on the table every single day. Here she was, struggling to put a smile on her face.

Vicky had to ask, "Bo, with no disrespect, how is it that you find it so easy to smile despite your current situation?"

Bo laughed. "You know thomething, mith...?"

"Muse. But please, call me Vicky."

"Okay, Vicky. I wathn't alwayth the happy camper you zee here today. I would beat mythelf up over everything. I wath alwayth the victim. Woe ith me. Everyone you zee here, all thethe homeleth folkth, have been there and probably thtill are. I realithed one day that if you thtep outthide yourthelf and look around, there ith alwayth, ALWAYTH, thomebody who'th worthe off than you. You don't even have to look very far either. I figured out that we all have choitheth. You can complain or you can trutht in God that there'th a reathon for everything."

"Yes, but-"

"I'm not going to be in thith thituation forever, Vicky. I know that for sure. God ith thtill working. You've got to let Him work. Every time thomething 'bad' happenth to uth, it ith usually a blesthing in dithguithe. Trutht Him! And when you feel that you have nothing left, give. Give, Vicky, give. That ith the key."

Everything Bo said made Vicky speechless. Deep down, she knew he was right. It really was a matter of where your focus was.

Amanda gave Bo the leftover food and Bo thanked her again for it.

"It was really nice to meet you, Bo," said Vicky.

"It was really nice to see you again, Bo," Amanda added.

"Thank you zo much, little lady. Coco and I shall featht tonight. Remember that I'll be here if you need me."

The mother and daughter duo went back home. Going to the park was therapeutic for Vicky. She never imagined that helping out a perfect stranger would give her so much gratification. It just made her problems seem a little bit smaller.

When she put things into perspective, it became easier for her to realize that her struggles weren't as bad as she was making them out to be. Vicky started to feel better about the news of her husband having a son. She even began embracing the idea of having another baby boy in her home. She genuinely started feeling enthusiastic about it. In fact, she started to plan in her mind how she was going to deliver the news to the rest of the family. Although she wanted to tell Amanda, she held her tongue and decided to wait until after she spoke to Eric again.

As they walked, Amanda said, "Thanks a lot, Mom. I felt really good bringing the food over to Bo and Coco."

"Sweetie, the pleasure was all mine. Thank you! Going over to see your friend was a very good idea."

"So if I wanted to walk the park after school, can I?"

"Now why would you want to take a longer route home, honey? It just doesn't make any sense!"

Amanda decided to fill her mother in about Mildred and Liz, about how she was intimidated by them, and about how Mildred had gotten suspended.

"What? Are you being bullied? Why didn't you tell me this before? Well, you don't worry about a thing, sweet pea. I'll be going to that school first thing Monday morning!"

"No, Mom, it's okay, really. Lucinda stood up to them and got the bigger girl, Mildred, suspended."

"What about the other girl, the not so big one?"

"Oh, she apologized. She would not dare do anything on her own. She needs her bodyguard."

"So what's the problem then, why the park?"

"Just to avoid them that's all. I can always tell a teacher in school and they'll protect me there, but outside of school is a different story. I would just rather avoid them."

"Okay, Amanda, if you feel that that's what you need to do, then do it. Have Bo walk you if he can, and if those girls continue giving you a hard time, you let me know. Okay, sweet pea?"

"Yes, Mom, I promise."

They finally got home and Vicky was eager to speak with her husband. She prepared the kids for bed a little early just to have that private time to talk with him. Once the kids were in bed, Vicky and Eric were alone once again in their bedroom.

"Hey, babe, how are you feeling?" said Eric. His concern and fear were obvious in his voice and the way that he stood.

"You know, Eric? Before I went for that walk, I wasn't sure what to think. I wasn't sure if divorcing you would solve anything."

"Babe, it wouldn't, I-"

"Please let me finish. I already forgave you for having the affair, and I guess this child is innocent and doesn't deserve to be punished for your actions."

"What are you saying, babe?"

With a big smile, Vicky turned to him. "I'm not saying anything. I'm asking you, when are we meeting our son?"

Eric fell to his knees crying. "Oh, babe, thank you so much!"

"Get up, Eric. I've always wanted another baby and now I have one. I will trust in God that this child will be a blessing to our home. So, how old is he? Do you know his name? When do we get to meet him?"

"His name is Kevin, Kevin Eng; but when we get custody, he will be Kevin Muse. He will be three in February, February fourteenth, actually, on Valentine's Day. If I start the paperwork, by Christmas break, I could go to New York and pick him up. It will be our Christmas gift, babe!" Eric was very excited. He was already planning how everything would go in the coming months.

Later, they told the rest of the family the good news. Everyone was happy and excited about the idea of having a new baby in the family. They were all beginning to fall in love with Kevin even though they had never met him. They couldn't wait to meet him.

After Vicky met Bo, dinner time was never the same. She always kept Bo in mind. Whenever she could, she would gather leftovers and walk over to the park, not only to feed Bo, but the other homeless people in the park as well. It brought her so much joy to give. Amanda would also go with her and it gave the two of them some quality time together. Their spirits were lifted every time they went, every single time.

CHAPTER 6

. . . .

Cyberbullying

*T*he air was tense at the Riley home. Joe had picked his daughter up from school and it was obvious that he had been drinking. The school staff seriously considered calling Child Protective Services to further investigate the matter, but they never got around to doing it. The staff could tell that Mildred was very embarrassed to have her drunk dad there. Thank goodness that none of the other students were there to witness it. Being a bully herself, Mildred knew that others would make fun of her for having her drunken father pick her up.

After picking Mildred up from school, Joe decided to take the rest of the day off. Once home, he continued to drink and man, did he get drunk! Mildred made him a sandwich before heading to her room. She was hoping that the sandwich would sober him up a bit or at least get him sleepy enough that he would go sleep off the alcohol. With the whole day ahead of him, Joe got bored and frustrated. He decided to drink some more.

After a while, he started to yell for his daughter. "Mildred! Mildred!"

"What is it, Dad?" She walked out of her room to talk to him.

"Why did you have to get suspended for? I had to waste a good day's work because of you!" Even though it was his choice not to return to work, he figured he'd blame Mildred for it. He had to blame somebody, and he sure as hell was not going to assume any responsibility for his actions.

"That was your choice, Dad. You could've gone back," said Mildred.

"Don't be a smartass with me, missy! I'll open a can of whooping on you! You hear me?"

Mildred sighed and walked back into her room. As soon as she walked in, she closed the door.

"Don't you close that door on me, missy!" Her father continued to shout.

Mildred ignored him. Joe might act like a fool most of the time, but he did respect the privacy of her room. In fact, Joe had never been inside Mildred's room. For some reason, he never crossed that line. It was Mildred's one safe place.

"If you continue to walk this path missy, you're going to end up in jail like your mama!" His shouts came from outside her door.

After saying that, he turned around and walked toward his room. Mildred was shocked by the words that he had said. All this time, the only thing she knew was that her mother left. Nobody knew where or why or at least that's what it had appeared to be. Her mother being in jail was news to her.

She quickly unlocked and opened the door. "Jail? What do you mean jail? You know where my mom is?"

Joe turned back to her. "Of course I know. I've always known! That no good loser is in the Women's Correctional Facility up in Denver where you'll be going if you don't get your act together!"

"But you never... You always told me that you had no idea where she was! How could you do that? How could you keep this from me?"

"What do you care anyway? She left us to be with some young buck. That was her choice! She is where she belongs! Now leave me alone. I'm going to sleep!"

This was such a blow for Mildred. She was so hurt, but also relieved. For as long as she could remember, Mildred thought her mother wanted nothing to do with her. It suddenly became clear why she had never heard from her mother.

Mildred had so many questions. However, she figured that it would be better to let her father sleep off the alcohol before she tried to ask him anything.

Mildred's home was probably the only home in Colorado that did not have Internet access. Joe Riley never saw the need for it. They owned a personal computer once, but it was so old that it started to act up. It would restart unexpectedly on its own. Sometimes, it turned on by itself in the middle of the night, scaring the bejesus out of Joe. It was as if the computer was possessed by a whole legion of demons. Ultimately, Joe got so frustrated with all the ticks it had that he just got rid of it.

Luckily, there was a public library nearby. Whenever Mildred needed the Internet for whatever reason, she would walk over to the library and use the Internet there. When Mildred woke up the following morning, she decided to go to the library and see if she could find out more information about her mother.

Coincidently, Amanda and her entire family needed to go to the library that day as well. Junior did not know how to use the computer. When it came to his school assignments, he needed to resort to more traditional methods. Naturally, when he had to go to the library, the whole family would go with him. Amanda's parents insisted on keeping things 'old school' and they encouraged their kids to visit the library. Usually, Eric looked at the section where the documentary DVDs were, while Vicky helped Junior look for the books he needed. While they were all busy, Amanda went to use the computer to check her email and social media.

Mildred, who was already in the library, noticed when the Muses came in. She was in the computer section trying to find out more information about her mother.

When she noticed that Amanda was heading to the computers, she quickly got into stealth mode and hid behind some bookshelves.

Isabel M. Peña

Mildred did not understand why, but she wanted to see what Amanda's personal life was like.

Mildred was always curious to know where Amanda's looks came from. Where Mildred grew up, people were either African American or White. Other races were practically non-existent. Interracial marriages in that part of town were simply unheard of. Mildred's world was so narrow that it never occurred to her that other races could actually mix.

Once Mildred got to see Amanda's family all together, it all started to make sense. In an odd way, she was fascinated by the family. She also noticed that Amanda's older brother, Junior, seemed to have special needs. This was very interesting to Mildred. All of this information was stuff that she could use against Amanda. Mildred was just loading up on ammunition.

After the Muses got everything that they needed from the library, they headed out. To Mildred's delight, Amanda forgot to log out of her Facebook account before she left. Mildred couldn't believe it! This was an early Christmas gift for Mildred.

As soon as it was safe to come out, Mildred went over to the computer Amanda had been using. There wasn't time to waste with this amazing gift. She wasn't sure of what she wanted to do with Amanda's account. One thing's for sure, Mildred hated Amanda more than ever. It just gnawed at her that Amanda lived in such a 'perfect' little world. It wasn't a world that Mildred could ever see herself living in.

Mildred was not very social-media savvy. She didn't even have a Facebook page herself. She was, however, familiar with how social media worked because that was all Liz ever talked about. Liz had made an account for Mildred once, but Liz ended up being Mildred's only friend. It was too depressing for Mildred because it became a constant reminder that she had no family or friends. Eventually, Mildred made Liz delete her account with the excuse that she didn't have a computer at home.

Mildred began snooping around Amanda's list of friends. Most of the list was filled with relatives. Amanda didn't have many friends from school on her Facebook, but she did have Lucinda, Daniel, and Sky. That was all that Mildred needed. She knew that even with only three friends from the same school, the entire student body would somehow be able to see her page and the posts.

Mildred decided to post on Amanda's timeline 'I'm in a relationship with - Lucinda Johnson.' She also tagged Lucinda so that her friends would be able to see the post as well. Not completely satisfied, she then posted, 'THAT'S RIGHT Y'ALL! I'M QUEER AND NOW I'M HERE!!!'

Mildred proceeded to log off. Feeling satisfied, she left the library. She had gotten such a thrill from messing with Amanda that she had forgotten why she was in the library in the first place. Mildred walked home calmly, like nothing had happened.

For the rest of that Saturday, Amanda spent it helping her brother with his school project. On Sundays, the Muses spent their day in church and with family. This meant that Amanda didn't get the chance to log onto her social media account till Monday.

Apparently, all of Amanda's family and friends were also too busy that weekend. No one noticed the status update until Monday morning. When Amanda returned to school, she realized almost immediately that something wasn't right. Some kids were laughing as she walked past them. Others gave her a bad look. When she got to her locker, she found a distraught Lucinda waiting for her. Amanda could tell that Lucinda was already ready for class, but she was just waiting for her. "Lucinda, can you tell me what the heck is going on?" Amanda said as she approached the locker.

"I was just about to ask you the same thing!" said Lucinda.

"What do you mean?"

"You posted on Facebook that we were in a relationship! Then you publicly came out! It sounds nothing like you, Mandy. What the hell are you thinking? Is this your idea of a joke?"

"What? Are you serious? I have no idea what you are talking about."

Deep down Lucinda did find it suspicious. She knew that this was not like Amanda at all. But if Amanda hadn't done it, then who else could have? Lucinda suggested that Amanda check her account before the entire school filled with rumors.

Suddenly, Sky came running toward them like a mad woman. "Oh my god! What the heck?"

"I know!" said Lucinda.

Amanda did not know what to say. She couldn't imagine who could have possibly tampered with her Facebook account. She had no idea why anybody would do something like that to her and Lucinda specifically.

Amanda turned to the girls. "Listen, you guys, I really don't know what is going on here. Obviously, someone is messing around with my account. I need to find out who, but the school library does not let us log on to our Facebook. The only thing I can tell you is that I didn't do it. As a matter of fact, I haven't used my Facebook since Saturday when I went to the public library to – Oh my god! I must have forgotten to log out!"

"I knew that couldn't be you!" said Sky.

"Well, you need to do something now! My friends and family could see this!" Lucinda was desperate to not face humiliation and questioning from everyone that she knew.

Amanda was at a loss. "But what could I do? I can't use the computer in school!"

"Let's go speak to somebody in the office. Maybe they can help," suggested Lucinda.

"Okay, let's go see what they tell us."

All three girls ran to the main office and explained the situation. Unfortunately, there was nothing they could do in school. The office staff advised Amanda to call her mother. There was a chance that Vicky would be able to fix things from home.

Amanda agreed and called Vicky. She asked her mother to please log into her account and write in the status bar how somebody had tampered with her account at the public library.

Ideally, this would have prevented rumors from spreading, but it looked like it was too late at Lakewood Junior High. The news had spread all over the school like the plague. Most kids were smart enough to know that this was not something that Amanda would do. Even Liz was finding it a little suspicious. She wondered if Mildred had anything to do with it. Messing with a Facebook account did seem like something that Mildred would do.

By the end of the school day, nobody knew for sure what had really happened. The topic became less interesting and less talked about. Had Mildred been at school, she would have fueled the rumors and kept them going. Without Mildred, the rest of the day went fairly quietly. By the time the day was over, everyone had forgotten all about it.

CHAPTER 7

....

Busted!

*N*othing big or bad came out of the cyberbullying incident. Amanda's rapport with others aided her in convincing other kids that none of it was true. Amanda was a very likable girl. The only girls that ever gave her any problems were Mildred and Liz, and that was because they were jealous of her. Everybody was still curious though. Finally, they all concluded that it was a random stranger at the public library trying to be funny, and who, coincidently, picked Lucinda out of Amanda's group of friends to be her significant other.

Thursday eventually rolled around and this meant that Mildred's suspension had been lifted. Mildred's dad had to leave town on one of his over–the-road routes toward South Dakota and was going to be gone for three days. He said his goodbyes and off he went.

Mildred returned to school and went straight to her locker. While she prepared for her class, Liz walked over to her to fill her in on everything that happened while she was out. Meanwhile, unbeknownst to them, Daniel was also by his locker preparing for his class. Daniel's locker was close enough to them that he could hear everything that Mildred and Liz were saying.

"Hey Mildred, did you hear?" said Liz practically glowing.

"Hear what?" said Mildred.

"Somebody was messing around with Bloody Mandy's Facebook account and posted on her status that she was a Lesbo in love with Lucinda."

After Liz was done telling Mildred the breaking news, Mildred giggled in an almost satanic way. She confessed to Liz, "I did that. I posted that on her status. The little twerp was in the library on Saturday. I saw her, but she didn't see me. When she left, the idiot left her Facebook page wide open. Psss! What a moron!"

Daniel looked up at the sound of this news, but quickly looked down to keep from being recognized. Mildred and Liz were so engaged in their conversation that they did not see him at all, even though he was only fifteen feet away.

"No way!" said Liz, "That was brilliant, Mildred!"

"I know! Wasn't it?"

"Well, sorry to tell you, but nothing came out of it. Nobody bought it, but if your goal was to torment them, it totally worked. Amanda and Lucinda were so freaked out. It was awesome!"

"Oh well, at least I tortured them in some way. Anything that makes their lives miserable, even if it's just for one second, makes me happy."

Mildred closed her locker and headed to class with Liz right beside her. Daniel stood there in shock. He was going to see the girls fourth period, but he couldn't wait. He ran as quickly as he could to the biology class where he knew he would find both Amanda and Lucinda. He also needed to get there before Mildred and Liz did.

Mildred and Liz always took their time to get to class. They always walked the hallways as if they were two jail wardens. Daniel felt confident he'd make it to the classroom first.

Daniel did make it to biology before Mildred and Liz. Even Mr. Erickson, the biology teacher, had not yet arrived. Mr. Erickson was scheduled to have his class dissect frogs and was waiting for somebody to open the lab refrigerator where the frogs were kept. Daniel quickly asked Amanda and Lucinda to step outside the classroom for a second.

Once they were out in the hallway, he started, "Hey dudettes! Quick, I gotta tell you something."

"What is it, dude?" said Lucinda.

"Yeah, dude, what is it?" said Amanda.

Out of breath, he said, "Listen, I was just in my locker minding my own business and I overheard Mildred telling Liz that she changed your status on Facebook!"

Amanda and Lucinda said at the same time, "What?"

"Yup," Daniel continued, "She said that she saw you, Amanda, at the library Saturday morning, but you didn't see her. When you left, she wrote on your timeline that thing about you and Lucinda being, you know… Anyway, after Liz told her that nothing came of it, Mildred said that she didn't care; that she was happy just making you guys miserable!"

After hanging out with girls for so long, Daniel had become quite the gossiper.

Shocked with the news, Lucinda launched one of her 'B' bombs. "That bitch! Just wait until I see her!"

"Leave it alone, Lucinda, just leave it alone! You are only going to make things worse. Besides, nothing came out of it," said Amanda, seeking only peace.

Lucinda was not having it though.

"Mandy, she is never going to stop unless we fight back! She was already suspended last week and she was given a warning. Maybe this time they will expel her for good!"

"Okay, dudettes, I gotta go," said Daniel. "I just came over to let you know." Then, he left.

The girls went back into their classroom. Amanda did not really want to get Mildred in trouble again. Amanda was raised by a family who believed that love, compassion, forgiveness, and patience was the cure for everything. As for Lucinda, she was more into what's right is right and what's wrong is wrong. She was not as passive as Amanda and she was determined to seek justice.

When biology class started, Lucinda asked Mr. Erickson if she could be excused. She told him that she needed to see the school counselor regarding an important and private matter. Since she put it in that way, he excused her from class with no questions asked.

Lucinda met with the school counselor, Mrs. Dotson, and told her everything in full detail. Lucinda and Amanda were in her office a few days before regarding this matter. Needless to say, Mrs. Dotson was well aware of the situation. Mrs. Dotson instructed Lucinda to go back to her classroom and reassured her that she would take it from there.

When Lucinda returned to the classroom, she noticed that Mildred was already there. Lucinda did not say anything and sat down. It was several periods later that Mrs. Dotson showed up to class to get Mildred. She just pulled Mildred out and took her straight to her office. Mildred was clueless as to what was going on. She assumed that Mrs. Dotson just wanted to speak to her about the events that led to her suspension the week before.

Mrs. Dotson did not waste any time. Immediately, she asked Mildred about her going into Amanda's Facebook page. Mildred was surprised that Mrs. Dotson suspected her of being the culprit. Mildred assumed right away that Liz must have said something because Liz was the only person who knew. Mildred couldn't believe that Liz would betray her in that way. It really didn't make any sense.

Surprisingly, Mildred did not deny anything. She was more concerned about how Mrs. Dotson found out. Mrs. Dotson reminded Mildred of the warning she had given her the last time she was suspended.

In a very disappointed voice, Mrs. Dotson said to her, "My dear child, what are we going to do with you? Why do you continue to do these things? Do you have anything to say in your defense?"

"I don't know, miss! I was angry because she got me suspended."

"Mildred, you got yourself suspended! Amanda did not do anything to you!"

"Then I guess it's because I hate her."

"But why? What has she done to you that has made you hate her?"

"I don't know, okay! I just do. She thinks she's so cute and perfect and it just irks me."

"Mildred, Amanda does not think any of those things. Apparently, you are the one who thinks those things about her."

"That's stupid! As a matter of fact, her family is weird. Her father's black, her mother is white, and she's got a retarded brother and everything. I saw them on Saturday in the library, her whole weirdo family was there."

Realizing that Mildred had deeper issues, issues that she would not be able to handle, Mrs. Dotson made the decision to expel Mildred from school until she underwent psychiatric evaluations. Mildred had gotten into trouble way too many times to ignore.

After a long exhale, Mrs. Dotson said, "Mildred, I hate to do this to you dear, but I am going to have to recommend that you'd be expelled from the school. I am really sorry, but I will be calling your dad to advise him on possible solutions. You need someone to help you deal with other people and with all these feelings that are festering inside."

What a blow this was for Mildred. She lost it. The idea of being stuck at home indefinitely really got to her. "This sucks! You guys and everybody here suck big time! I hope some terrorist comes here and bombs this stupid school and everybody dies! I hate you all!"

Mrs. Dotson, not wanting to add more fuel to the fire, didn't say another word. She just took a deep breath, got up, and escorted Mildred back to her classroom to get her things.

When they returned to the classroom, Mildred turned to Amanda and said, "You are a zebra and you belong in a zoo with the rest of your zebra family!"

"That's enough, Mildred!" said Mrs. Dotson.

Completely ignoring Mrs. Dotson, Mildred turned to Liz. "And you, Liz, you are so dead!"

"What? What did I do?" said Liz.

"You know damn right what you did, you back stabbing snitch! I will get you back Liz, I swear to God I will get you back!"

"I said that's enough, Mildred!" said Mrs. Dotson.

"Hey, Oreo," Mildred continued looking straight at Amanda and walking toward the door, "I'm not done with you yet! Do you hear me, Stripes? I'll get you too!"

When Mildred was done getting all of her belongings and letting some steam out, she was escorted back to Mrs. Dotson's office where she waited for the school to call her father. Once they had Joe on the phone, Joe explained that he was somewhere near South Dakota and that he would not be getting home anytime soon. He told them that he would make arrangements to have Alice, his neighbor, pick Mildred up.

Alice was never busy and she arrived at the school rather quickly. She got Mildred and took her home. As always, Alice reminded Mildred to call her if she needed anything. Alice was very sweet.

It was still early and Mildred had the whole day ahead of her. Mildred decided to make herself something to eat. There was never a lot of food in Mildred's home, but she did find a can of spaghetti that was about to expire. It was not your typical homemade meal, but at least she was happy that her father was not home. She watched some television for a while and after a few hours, she got bored. Mildred needed to find something to do to help her kill some time, but she didn't feel like staying home. She decided to go hang out at Lakewood Park.

CHAPTER 8

●●

Rude Awakenings

The school day came to an end and Amanda was still shaken by Mildred's words from that morning. She felt the need to talk to Bo about her day. Amanda decided to go see Bo. Mildred was still in the park, and when Amanda arrived at the park, Mildred spotted her right away. Mildred was hesitant to start any trouble because there were people around, so she discretely followed Amanda. She had become so obsessed with Amanda that she was borderline stalking her. Mildred made sure that Amanda did not see her while she walked.

When Amanda got to Bo's camping tent, she found Bo crying hysterically. Amanda had never seen a grown man bawling the way he was.

She immediately reached out to him. "Bo, Bo, are you okay? What's the matter?"

Bo looked up at Amanda. "Oh, little lady, she'th gone, my Coco ith gone! I found her dead thith morning. Animal control jutht came and took her away. My heart ith broken into a million pieceth. I feel like I jutht got run over by a buth!"

"Oh, Bo, I am so sorry!" said Amanda, feeling Bo's pain.

"I don't know what I am going to do without her. She wath all I had."

"I really am sorry, Bo."

Bo tried to collect himself. He was actually glad that Amanda had stopped by. It was nice to have someone to share the pain with.

As he wiped his tears, he said, "What are you doing here anyway? Did you thomehow zenthe that I wath in dithtreth?"

"I really don't know, Bo. There was a problem today at school with the bully I spoke to you about and I needed someone to talk to."

"Oh, little lady, you know I'm alwayth here for you. It'th jutht that today I'm feeling, well, numb, I gueth."

"It's okay, Bo, I understand. I am also very sad that Coco is gone," Amanda said as she placed her hand on Bo's shoulder.

Mildred had been hiding nearby listening to Bo and Amanda's conversation. She couldn't believe that Amanda would talk to homeless people. Not only did she pick up that Bo was homeless, she was also able to pick up that he was a little bit on the feminine side.

All of a sudden, Mildred jumped out from where she was hiding, and started with her usual trash talking.

"Well, well, well, look who we have here. If it ain't Bloody Mandy and her stinky boyfriend," she said as she walked toward them.

"Uff!" She waved her hand in front of her nose as she continued. "Seems like somebody's 'Right Guard' just took a left turn!"

"Mildred? What are you doing here?" Amanda was surprised to see her in the park.

"You got me expelled remember? I have a lot of free time now thanks to you!"

"Mildred, I—"

"Shut up, Oreo! Does your zebra family know you talk to gay bums? Is that your boyfriend or something? He looks gay to me."

"Mildred, stop it!" Amanda yelled in frustration, "Why do you do this? Why do you say these things? Why do you hate me so much when you don't even know me? You don't even know him either! Why don't you just leave us alone? Leave *me* alone for once, please!"

"You are so pathetic, Stripes! I hate you just because you are you! I hate you because you were born! And I hate your boyfriend there because he's a dirty, smelly, gay bum!"

Amanda stood there in sheer dismay. She couldn't understand how some people could be so cruel for no reason. Feeling Amanda's pain as well as his own, Bo went stiff with anger. Bo had never met Mildred, but he quickly realized that this was the bully that had been tormenting his friend, Amanda.

Mildred had picked the wrong day to bully Amanda in Bo's presence. Maybe on another day, Bo would have been patient and constructive, but this was not that day.

Bo had been bullied all of his life for his weight, speech impediment, and mannerisms. Even though Bo had never been married, nobody really knew what his sexual orientation was. He had a girlfriend once when he was sixteen. She was the daughter of his Uncle Charlie's friend. His Uncle Charlie thought it would be a good idea to hook them up since he noticed that Bo was displaying some signs of homosexuality due to his mannerisms. The truth of the matter was, Bo's sexuality was a mystery. The way Bo felt about the subject was that it really wasn't anybody's business whom he chose (if he had a choice at all) to fall in love with.

Unfortunately, Bo's mannerisms got him a good dose of bullying even by his own family members. It didn't matter that he was a tall person. The only people who didn't make a big deal about it were his mother and his Uncle Charlie.

Bo was an only child and his mother doted on him. His father, on the other hand, was rather cold and disconnected. At times, Bo's father was embarrassed by Bo. When he died, it did not make much of a difference to Bo. His mother gave him enough love for both parents and he always had his Uncle Charlie to look up to as a paternal figure. It was too bad that his Uncle Charlie lived in Toronto with his wife because Bo could have used his support.

Still, Bo was fed up with people mistreating others for no reason. He was fed up with watching people suffer for being different or for something they had no control over. He just about had it with the small-minded and the ignorant who expect the world to be just like them as if they were perfect. For Bo, the only perfection was God, who loves us all unconditionally, and his beloved Coco.

All these feelings rushed into his very core and quickly grew. Everything that was happening to him that day and everything bad that had ever happened to him in all of his life, came crashing in. He thought of every bully that ever bullied him, and how Coco, which was the only thing that mattered to him, was gone.

Bo began to feel the anger, and even though it was out of character for him, he got mad. He got up and saw that there was a rock the size of an orange on the ground. He picked up the rock and without hesitation, nor any regard for consequences, he flung the rock at Mildred. The rock hit her right on the head. In an instant, she fell unconscious to the ground. As Mildred lay unconscious on the ground with blood gushing out of the right side of her head, Amanda stood there in complete shock and disbelief.

"Oh my god, Bo! What did you do?" Amanda said frantically.

Bo did not answer. He did not say a single word. He quietly turned around and walked slowly into his tent as if he didn't want to be bothered. Amanda looked around and luckily, there wasn't anybody there who saw Bo throw the rock.

Amanda knew that she needed to get help for Mildred. After a few moments, she saw that there was a woman jogging their way. When the woman was close, Amanda called on the woman for help. She felt scared and desperate.

"Help, somebody, please! Ma'am, please call an ambulance!"

The woman stopped and asked Amanda, "What happened? What's going on here?"

"A rock! Somebody threw a rock at her!" said Amanda scared out of her mind.

"A rock? Who threw the rock?" asked the lady.

"I don't know. It could've been anybody! Or maybe it fell! Yeah, I think it fell! A big rock fell and hit her head! A falling rock hit her! It came down that big boulder there."

Amanda pointed at a huge boulder that was close by in efforts to convince the lady that it was an accident and protect her friend

Bo. Amanda knew that Bo didn't mean to hurt Mildred. Mildred just caught him at a bad time.

"Oh my," said the woman, "People never think these things can happen, but they do."

The woman reached for her phone with one hand. With the other hand, she reached for the towel she had in her back pocket. She tried to wipe some of the blood that was gushing out of Mildred's head.

"Here, press on her head to try and stop the bleeding," she instructed Amanda.

The woman called 911 and an ambulance arrived in a matter of minutes. The paramedics took Mildred to the nearest hospital. Amanda tried to say goodbye to Bo, but he was not responding at all. He did not want to hear anything at that moment. Amanda gave up on Bo and ran home where she told her mother everything. Amanda convinced Vicky to take her to the hospital to see how Mildred was doing. Vicky agreed to go without giving it a second thought.

When Vicky and Amanda got to the hospital, the only thing that the hospital staff was able to tell them was that Mildred had been unconscious and that they needed to run some tests. The hospital staff was happy to see Amanda because she could give them more information about Mildred. The hospital staff had not been able to contact anybody who knew Mildred. They didn't even know what her name was. Fortunately, Amanda was able to provide them with Mildred's name and the school she attended. They could always call the school to find out who her parents were. The problem was that the school was closed at that time. They would have to wait until the next day to find out more information about Mildred or at least until she regained consciousness.

Amanda and Vicky sat in the waiting area for a long time. After a while, Vicky got tired of waiting. She turned to Amanda. "Honey, we have to go. We can come back tomorrow and find out how she's doing. I'm sure they'll know something by then."

"Oh Mom, just a little bit longer, please! Give them ten more minutes, please! If in ten minutes we don't hear from them, we'll leave okay?"

"Okay, ten more minutes, but that's it."

"Thanks, Mom!"

Two minutes later, a doctor came out and approached them.

"Hi, my name is Dr. Ross. Are you guys here for the young lady with the head injury?"

Vicky placed her hand on Amanda's shoulder and said, "Yes, we are. Hi, I'm Vicky and this is my daughter, Amanda. How is the young lady?"

"I'm sorry, but how are you related to her?" asked Dr. Ross.

Before Vicky said anything, Amanda quickly said, "She's a friend from school. I mean, she's not a 'friend' friend, but I do know her from school. I was there when she got hit on the head. Is she going to be okay?"

Letting out a long exhale and arming himself with courage, Dr. Ross said, "Well, she is. We have treated her wound and on a superficial level, it was less serious than it looked. We gave her five stitches and it should heal fairly quickly. There is, however, some bad news. This young lady appears to be suffering from retrograde amnesia. This type of amnesia is often caused by an injury or brain trauma. Basically, the patient is unable to remember any events that occurred before the amnesia set in. However, anything that happens after the injury is remembered normally. Unfortunately, she has no idea who she is, where she lives or who her parents are. So if you have any information regarding this patient, I ask that you please let our staff know."

After listening to the doctor, Amanda was speechless.

"Oh dear!" said Vicky concerned, "Will she ever recover her memory?"

"At this time, it's hard to tell. In most cases, complete memory can be restored and it can happen at any time. What she needs right now from her family and friends is patience. Amnesia can easily go on for months. Many times, a major or familiar event can bring memories back, resulting in a full recovery."

"Can we go see her?" asked Amanda.

"Actually, we will be observing her a bit longer and then she needs to rest. I just want to make sure that everything else internally is okay. If at all possible, please come back tomorrow. She will be well rested then."

"We will do just that. Thank you so much, Dr. Ross," said Vicky. "Come on, honey, we'll be back tomorrow."

Amanda and Vicky went home. On the way, Amanda pleaded with her mother to let her skip school the next day. She explained how much this meant to her. She also told her that the following day would be a Friday and according to Amanda, they never did anything big or bad in school on Fridays. Amanda also begged her mother not to say anything about Bo hitting Mildred with a rock, which Vicky agreed to do. Vicky also had grown to love Bo and knew that he would never deliberately hurt anybody.

When they got home, the little wheels in Amanda's head started to turn. Maybe this wasn't such a bad situation after all. Maybe this was a blessing in disguise. Amanda knew she could go many places with this, but she didn't know where.

Amanda's dad always told her that in life there are always at least two roads to take and that she should always take the one that would take her the farthest and lead her closer to God, who is love. She never understood what that meant, but she began to understand it at that moment.

There were three things that she could do. For one, she could let this whole incident go, pretend it never happened, and go on with her life as usual. Mildred got what she deserved and it really didn't matter what happened to her. She was expelled from school, and Amanda would probably never hear from her again.

This, of course, was the easy way out. If Amanda wanted to take her father's advice, this was definitely not the road to take. It was way too short and it would never get her anywhere near God.

The second thing she could do was to turn the tables on Mildred. She could probably convince Mildred that nobody likes her and that she is a victim of bullying. Amanda could even come up with other mean things just to get back at her. Since Mildred couldn't remember a thing, she would most likely be able to return to school. Amanda was sure that Mrs. Dotson would consider that. After all, Mildred probably forgot how mean and nasty she was to everybody else. The only problem with this was that if Mildred was to get her memory back, and chances were that she would, it would probably backfire on Amanda.

Amanda's last option was to maybe convince Mildred that they were both best friends. She could even tell Mildred that everyone loves her because she is such a loving and caring individual. After all, Amanda was convinced that Mildred never knew what it was like to be loved. If Mildred ever got her memory back, then it wouldn't matter because she was loved.

This road seemed just right. Everything about it seemed perfect. Mildred had to have some good in her. Maybe, if she was shown love and compassion, she'd change.

Bo once told Amanda that if she couldn't think of anything nice to say about someone, she was not thinking hard enough. Well, Amanda did a whole lot of thinking that day. Although Mildred had not been the nicest person, Amanda was sure that there had to be something nice about her. It just didn't make any sense that someone could have so much hate and anger in them. It had to come from somewhere. People aren't born hateful, angry babies.

This option felt right all over. It even gave Amanda goose bumps. Amanda became really psyched and decided that this was what she was going to do. Clearly, this road would take her the farthest and closer to God. Before embarking on this adventure though, Amanda had a little prep work to do.

The first thing that Amanda needed to do was to convince everyone in the school, including Mrs. Dotson, of her plan. She could get Lucinda to be a spokesperson for her. Lucinda was much more persuasive. Then, Amanda would go visit Mildred at the hospital and convince Mildred that they were best friends. It sounded simple enough.

Amanda was so excited at this point that she shared the news with her mother. Vicky, although a little unsure, had to admit that it was not such a bad idea. She was very proud of her daughter for always seeking a way to make the best peace. She assured Amanda that she would support her every step of the way.

Meanwhile, at the hospital, Mildred had woken up to a complete blur. Not only did she not know who she was nor what she was doing in a hospital, but the little she did know, was somewhat depressing.

There was a little boy in the room right across from her and it was always filled with family members and friends. She didn't know why the little boy was there, but it was obvious that he had many people who cared about him. Mildred wondered who her parents were and why they weren't there beside her.

Finally, she got a visit from Dr. Ross who tried to explain everything he thought happened to her as far as the accident. He explained that they were unable to contact her parents because they were still investigating who they were. He also mentioned that she did have one friend who was very concerned about her and would be coming back to see her the following day.

Somewhere near South Dakota, Joe was doing his route as usual. This time, he had begun drinking on the job. This was not usually the case for Joe. He always waited till he got home to drink, but things started to spiral out of control and his drinking habit was taking a turn for the worse. He began drinking during the day and on the job.

Driving under the influence of alcohol, Joe was swaying his truck from side to side, endangering the lives of many innocent people. Shortly after, a state trooper noticed the unstable truck and pulled him over. Deep down, Joe knew he had gone too far and that he needed help. Joe didn't even try to justify himself. He was very honest with the officer and admitted to driving under the influence. Joe had finally reached rock bottom. He was arrested and charged with a DUI.

While in the police station, Joe began to sober up. He needed to call Mr. Jackson, his boss, to tell him what happened. Mr. Jackson was a nice and decent man. He knew Joe for a long time and knew that Joe had been struggling, but despite the struggles, Joe had been faithful, responsible, and a hard worker.

Mr. Jackson felt compelled to help Joe. He immediately came to Joe's rescue and bailed him out. He told Joe that if he wanted to keep his job, he would have to submit himself into a ninety-day rehabilitation program. Once Joe completed the program, he would be able to return to work as usual. There was no question on Joe's mind that this was what he needed to do, if not for him, for his daughter.

The next call that Joe made was to Mildred. He needed to explain to her his situation. He called home, but there was no answer. He always kept his neighbor Alice's number on him just in case. He had also given Alice a copy of his apartment key in case he ever needed her to go in and check up on Mildred.

Since Mildred did not pick up the phone, Joe called Alice to go check on his daughter. Alice went into his apartment and there was nobody there. Joe became very concerned. His daughter might be a little brat at times, but she barely left the house. Besides, where would she go? Mildred really didn't have any friends, and Liz never invited Mildred over to her house.

Joe told Alice where he was and why. He told her that he would talk to the police to see if they could send someone over to his apartment. Joe asked Alice to please wait for them there and that he would try to call her back.

Joe explained his situation at home to the police. They promised to 'check it out.' Officers were sent to the Rileys' apartment where Alice was waiting. Right away, they began to investigate Mildred's whereabouts. The hospital was the first place that they checked, so it did not take long for the police to find her.

Hospital staff told the police that a thirteen-year-old Mildred Riley was there being treated for a head injury. They explained that the young lady had no recollection of who she was because she was suffering from amnesia. Police immediately notified Joe who was still at the station waiting to be released. He desperately wanted to get back home and see Mildred, but he was miles away. It was going to take him at least a day to get back.

Amanda woke up bright and early the following day. She was very eager to get her plan into effect. She thought she'd see Mildred first thing, but decided to stop by the school instead and let everyone in on the plan before talking to Mildred.

When she got to school at around 10:00 a.m., the first person she went to see was Mrs. Dotson. After explaining to Mrs. Dotson why she was not in school that day, she told Mrs. Dotson about her plan to befriend Mildred and have her believe that Mildred Riley was the best thing since people started chocolate covering everything. Amanda explained how this would give Mildred a chance to a bright new start. Surprisingly, the only concern that Mrs. Dotson had was about what would happen if Mildred recovered her memory one day. However, Amanda was able to convince Mrs. Dotson that by the time Mildred recovered, Mildred would have grown to know and accept her.

"I commend you, young lady, I really do," said Mrs. Dotson. "I commend you for seeking peace and giving somebody the opportunity to see life in a different way. I will allow Mildred Riley to return to school, but that is all I will do for you.

Being that she's lost her memory, I'm willing to give her the benefit of the doubt.

You do the rest and I'll pretend I know nothing of this, deal?"

"Deal! Thank you, Mrs. Dotson! Thank you!" said Amanda, feeling animated.

Amanda waited for the recess bell to ring so that she could meet with her friends. After the bell rang, she ran to the cafeteria to meet with Lucinda, Daniel, and Sky at their usual spot. Amanda told them everything that happened the day before except for the part where Bo threw a rock at Mildred. Amanda kept the falling rock story till the end.

"Oh my god!" said Sky, "Is Mildred going to speak with an English accent now?"

"No! What the heck are you talking about, Sky?" said Amanda.

"Haven't you heard of people getting whacked on the head and when they come to, they are speaking a foreign language or with a foreign accent?"

"Sky, stop talking crazy!" said Lucinda, "Amanda, I don't know about this."

At first, Lucinda was a little hesitant to go with the plan. Everyone else thought it was brilliant. Lucinda didn't see why Amanda wanted to help someone who had been so awful to her. In the end, everyone agreed that seeking revenge was not going to solve anything and it would just make matters worse. This was a golden opportunity to do some good and finally have peace in school.

"What about Liz, Amanda? What are we going to do about Liz?" asked Sky.

"I guess we need to talk to her too. If she agrees, we are good to go," said Amanda.

"Good luck with that," said Lucinda.

The hopeful quartet went to find Liz. They spotted her sitting by herself in the school yard, playing with her cell phone. When Amanda and her friends approached Liz and told her that her friend Mildred was in the hospital, there was very little reaction from Liz. It seemed as if she didn't even care that her 'buddy' was ill.

It was no surprise to anybody. Everyone knew that Liz only hung out with Mildred because she was afraid of her. As far as their friendship, Liz decided that it was best to follow the old saying, 'It is better to be the right hand of the devil than in his path.'

Amanda told Liz of what her intentions were. For the first time, Amanda was stern and determined. She felt very passionate about this.

Immediately, Liz got up. "Buzz off, Bloody Mandy! When Mildred gets out, I'm telling her everything you losers are planning to do."

"Listen, Bacardi!" said Lucinda out of nowhere.

"It's Lombardi, methane!" responded Liz.

"What-ever, Lamborghini, you have the most to gain out of this. Are you forgetting that Mildred wants to kick your ass for snitching on her about the whole Facebook incident and for getting her kicked out of school?"

"I didn't do anything! Besides, she won't even remember a thing." said Liz.

"Oh yeah, dimwit? Well, we will make sure to remind her," argued Lucinda.

There was very little to say or do at that point. Liz was stuck. She was petrified of Mildred, and if she was unable to convince Mildred that she had nothing to do with her getting kicked out of school, she would be, as Mildred warned her, 'dead.'

"All right, losers," said Liz, "What do you want me to do?"

"Ok, from now on, Mildred is *our* friend," said Amanda. "We will tell her that she is far from being a bully; that she is the nicest girl in the school and that everybody loves her. What you can do is to simply stay out of it. Can you do that, Liz?"

"Fine, now let me be! Go about your business and leave me alone," said Liz as she went back to her phone.

With Mrs. Dotson and Liz out of the way, convincing everyone else was a piece of cake. Not only was everyone in agreement, but everyone was eager to get the plan going. Everything was falling into place. Amanda was convinced that God was on her side and that everything would work in her favor. Then, she went off to the hospital.

"When the power of love overcomes the love of power, the world will know peace."

- Jimi Hendrix

CHAPTER 9

The Good News

Amanda ran home. She needed to ask Vicky to take her to the hospital. Joe was also on his way. Mildred was still in the hospital alone, wondering where her 'loved ones' were. Vicky and Amanda arrived at the hospital first and were finally allowed to see Mildred. Amanda was feeling a bit nervous. She wondered if Mildred would recognize her despite the amnesia. Still, Amanda gathered up the courage to go see her.

When Vicky and Amanda went into Mildred's room, they noticed that Mildred had a dazed look on her face. They could tell that although she had no idea who was in her room, she was at least glad to have someone finally come see her.

"Hi, Mildred, how are you doing, buddy?" said Amanda.

"Hi, I feel fine. Who are you?" said Mildred.

Being that Amanda looked so different from Vicky, Mildred turned to Vicky and asked her, "Are you my mom?"

"No, sweetheart, I am Amanda's mom," said Vicky.

"Who's Amanda?"

Amanda's heart pounded with excitement.

She cleared her throat. "I'm Amanda. I'm your best friend. How are you?"

At that moment, Mildred did not feel so unloved. Vicky politely excused herself to let the girls talk, but before leaving she said, "Amanda, I'm going to get a coffee. Do you girls want anything?"

"Yeah, Mom, bring me a Snickers bar and Milly would like her usual."

"What's my usual?"

"Twix, of course," said Amanda taking a wild guess. She figured, who doesn't like Twix?

"Twix? Okay, I guess."

As soon as Vicky left, Mildred turned her attention back to Amanda. "So, best friends, huh?"

"Yup, BFFs!" said Amanda practically glowing.

"What's a BFF?"

"Best friends forever, silly!"

"Oh, okay. I was starting to feel like an outcast. By the way, where are my parents?"

"I don't know. They'll be here soon I'm sure."

"What happened to me?"

"Well, we were walking home from school and a big rock fell on your head."

"Where did the rock fall from?"

"Oh, from bigger rocks in the park. Lakewood Park has many big, red rocks and they often fall down. There are signs everywhere warning people and stuff, but I guess nobody pays much attention to them."

"How long have we been friends?"

"Well, not too long. Since school started in August. We just clicked right away. We've been inseparable ever since."

"What day is today?"

"Today is Friday. Friday, the Eighth of November, 2013."

"Wow. I don't remember anything. The doctor told me that my name is Mildred. Mildred Rrr...?"

"Riley. Your name is Mildred Riley."

"Yeah, Riley. Gosh, this is crazy! I don't remember anything."

"Don't worry. You'll be okay. I will help you remember some stuff. It's going to take a little time though. You are just going to have to be patient, that's all."

"I know. That's what the doctor told me."

"Hey, at least you're not talking in another language or in a weird English accent like Sky thought."

"Who's Sky?"

"She's just a friend of ours from school."

"Oh, okay."

Vicky got her coffee and some snacks for the girls. She began to walk back to the room. On her way, she came across a frantic Mr. Joe Riley.

"Where is she?" he asked the staff. "Where's my daughter, Mildred Riley? She was brought here yesterday and she—"

"She's right over in this room," interrupted Vicky.

She gently pulled him aside to introduce herself and fill him in on what had happened. As soon as Vicky began to talk, one of the nurses called Joe and told him that Dr. Ross wanted to speak with him. Dr. Ross approached Joe and told him basically everything he told Vicky and Amanda. This time, he added that Mildred would have to be carefully monitored and cared for. He also added that a stress-free environment would be best for her.

Joe was very bummed out about this. The only thing he was good at was providing a roof over their heads and food on the table. To make matters worse, he had a ninety-day program he needed to attend in order to be able to work and regain his life.

This was too much for him to bear. Joe Riley was a strong man, but he found himself not being able to hold the pieces together. He just sat down on the nearest chair and started to cry. He broke down harder than he'd ever had. This was where Joe had reached his breaking point. He cried like a ten-year-old boy.

Naturally, it broke Vicky's heart to see him in that way. Vicky was the type of person who couldn't see other people cry, especially a grown man. Dr. Ross excused himself and left them alone. Vicky sat right beside Joe trying to console him.

She placed her hand on his shoulder and said, "Mr. Riley, I don't know you or what's going on with you or your family situation at home, but things always work out in the end. Give it some time."

"You don't understand, ma'am, I cannot care for her. I cannot care for my own daughter; not by myself, not right now."

"Mr. Riley, I don't mean to pry, but where's Mrs. Riley?"

"She left. She left us a couple of years ago to be with someone else. She got into some trouble with the law and is now serving time in jail."

Vicky could tell that he was embarrassed.

"But that's not even the issue right now," he continued, "I have some problems of my own. I've been drinking a lot and I was just charged with a DUI. I need help. If I don't do something right now, I am only going to get worse. This is not what I want, not for me, not for Mildred. I know I can do this, I know I can change, but I need to make sacrifices and I need some help. I can't do this alone. I'm supposed to go away for about three months, but I don't know what to do with Mildred."

"Is there anybody, maybe a family member who can help you with her?"

"No, there isn't. The only person we know is my next-door neighbor, Alice, and she is too old to care for a rebellious thirteen-year-old girl. I can't do that to her."

Joe's situation touched Vicky's heart. She felt that if she didn't help one way or another, two lives would be ruined forever. How could she just sit there and pretend that this was none of her business? Three months go by so fast. Three months mean so little to her and yet so much for these two people.

The bigger question for Vicky was: would she be able to live with herself if she didn't help this family? Vicky did not have the heart to do that. She knew that if she did not lend a helping hand, this would make her a bitter and miserable woman. She would have guilt and regret in her heart forever.

Vicky turned completely toward Joe, looked him straight in the eyes and said, "Mr. Riley, I realize we've just met, but do you trust me?"

"How do you mean, Mrs…?"

"Call me Vicky, please. Do you trust me with your daughter?"

"I don't understand. What are you getting at?"

"Look, Mr. Riley—"

"Call me Joe, please."

"Joe. The truth is that my daughter, Amanda, has been bullied by your daughter since school started. Her response to all of this is to take advantage of the fact that Mildred does not remember any of it and try to convince her that they are actually best friends. Amanda is not doing this because she is afraid of your daughter, but because she believes that there has to be some good in Mildred. She believes that if Mildred is shown goodness and love, she can become a healthy and loving person."

"I'm so sorry, I had no idea," said Joe.

"Let Mildred stay with us, in our home, till you are done with your program. This would give you some time to sort yourself out and it would also allow Mildred to kind of 'reset' herself as well. There is really nothing to lose here Joe, but a whole lot to gain."

"Are you sure, Vicky? I really don't want to impose."

"It would be my pleasure, Joe. Don't you worry about a single thing. Your daughter will be in good hands and well taken care of. The only thing you need to worry about right now is making it right. Make it right for you and make it right for your daughter."

"I don't know what to say, Mrs. Vicky. Thank you. Thank you so much and may God bless you."

"There's one thing that you can do for me, Joe."

"What is that?"

"Just go along with my daughter's story that she and Mildred are good friends."

"No problem, ma'am. Your daughter is wise beyond her years. I believe she's right. It's hard, you know, being a single dad and all. I guess women are better at showing all that love and affection stuff, you know what I mean?"

"Well, Joe, we as parents do the best that we can with what we know. C'mon, let's go check on the girls."

Joe and Vicky went to the room and were pleasantly surprised to see the girls chatting and laughing away. They really did click and hit it off. Amanda told Mildred stories of their friends at school and how much fun they have together. Mildred was almost looking forward to going back to school and 'reuniting' with her friends.

"Hey, baby girl, how are you?" said Joe.

"Baby girl? Does that mean you're my dad?"

"I sure am. Do you remember me?"

"I'm sorry, sir, but I don't."

"Oh, that's all right. The doctor said that it'll take you some time. You'll be all right. And who do you have here with you?"

Amanda could hear her heart pounding in her ears. She gave Vicky a look that only a puppy would give its owner after they have torn up the house. Vicky placed her hand on Amanda's shoulder, smiled, and gave her a reassuring look.

"This is Amanda. She's my friend," said Mildred.

Joe looked at Amanda and reassured her by giving her a wink. Amanda looked at her mom with a sigh of relief. Then the room went silent. Joe looked at Vicky and she understood that he needed a moment alone with his daughter. Vicky grabbed Amanda's hand and told her to give them some time alone.

Once alone, Joe turned a bit more serious. This was the beginning of the rest of their new lives. Joe was feeling pretty good about it too. He felt that in order to do things right, he'd have to come clean about everything, and he did.

He told Mildred everything. He told her about her mom and how she had abandoned them and that he was raising her all by himself. He confessed how hard it had been for him as a single dad, so much so that he began to abuse alcohol to the point of becoming an alcoholic. He explained that he wanted and needed to turn his life around for everyone's sake, and that she would have to stay with her friend Amanda for a little while. Joe told Mildred that even though their lives were not nearly as perfect, he promised that it would be a whole lot better from there on.

Mildred was completely lost. She had no idea what was going on, and she had no other choice but to trust him. What else could she do? At least she liked Amanda so far, and her mother, Vicky, seemed very nice as well.

Vicky told Amanda the good news of Mildred moving in for a while. Amanda was so excited she couldn't wait. She had such a good feeling about it. It was like having the sister she always wanted.

Joe went to speak with the doctor and to sign the discharge papers. He was instructed to bring Mildred back in two weeks to follow up and remove her stitches. Amanda and Vicky went back to say their farewells and told Mildred that they will see her again very soon.

After leaving the hospital, Joe and Mildred went home to make the necessary arrangements for Mildred to move in with Amanda and her family. Joe also needed to prepare for when he left to get his treatment. He spoke to Alice so that she would keep an eye on their place while they were both out.

Vicky and Amanda had to get things ready at their end also. Vicky had not spoken to her husband about moving Mildred in, but she knew that it would not be a problem. Eric was a very laid-back and easygoing kind of guy who would do anything for his family. Besides, after that illegitimate son card that he had pulled on Vicky, he would be very eager to please her in any way that he could.

Once home, Vicky and Amanda anxiously waited for Eric. While they waited, Amanda, Vicky, and Amanda's Aunt, Ivette, who was there watching Junior, started to organize Amanda's room. There was not much that needed to be done. Amanda had a day bed and it had another twin mattress underneath it that could easily be pulled out. The only thing they needed to do was create closet space for some of Mildred's belongings and they did that fairly quickly.

Finally, Eric arrived. After complaining about a long day's work and how he was looking to hire someone to help out at work, Vicky invited him over to the family room where she instructed him to have a seat.

It looked serious, so he immediately asked her, "Victoria, what is going on?"

"Nothing," said Vicky with a smile on her face.

"Oh man, babe, the last time you had that look on your face, you told me that you were pregnant," said Eric, concerned.

"Don't be silly! I just wanted you to know that I offered to care for Amanda's friend for a little while: three months, perhaps."

"What? What friend? Why?"

"Look, it's a long story but basically, Amanda's friend, Mildred, from school, had an accident which caused her to lose her memory. Her dad is unable to care for her right now so I offered to help. I just wanted to see if it was okay with you."

"Babe, a man is only as strong as the woman who holds him, and I am a very strong man. I trust you and this is one of the many reasons why I love you so much. Of course, it's okay."

"Oh, thank you, honey. You're the best!"

With that, it was all settled. Now it was just a matter of waiting for Mildred to arrive. Joe promised to bring Mildred the following day so he can fix things up at his end.

Early Saturday morning, Joe took Mildred to the Muses'. Everybody was happy to have Mildred there. Joe told Mildred that he would not be able to speak to her for the first three weeks of the program because this was something that the program required in order to avoid any distractions. They would, however, be able to speak after three weeks.

It was all the same to Mildred at that point. She really didn't know anybody well enough to miss them. She was feeling a bit frustrated because she didn't remember anyone, but at least she embraced her new but temporary family and was eager to get to know them better.

CHAPTER 10

· ·

A Whole Different Story

*T*he first day at the Muses was basically getting to know everyone, establishing routines, and distributing chores. Amanda and Mildred spent a lot of time together, talking about everything. They were getting along so well. Amanda informed Mildred about their other friends at school. She spoke about Lucinda, Daniel, and Sky and how they all hung out. Amanda was gradually throwing names around to see if any of them would ring a bell. To her relief, Mildred did not have a clue about any of them. Amanda even mentioned Liz and nothing happened.

Mildred also became very drawn to Junior. She felt compassion and love towards him; not in a physical way, but as a sibling. It was unbelievable. It was as if Mildred had been given a new heart. Not for one second did she feel the urge to make fun of Junior for being special or Amanda for coming from such a unique family. On the contrary, she felt humbled by their kindness and was happy to be there.

Throughout the day, Amanda and Mildred were becoming so comfortable with each other that they began to call each other 'Milly' and 'Mandy.' Mildred even started calling Vicky 'Mrs. V.' Vicky was very happy to see them together and Amanda was thrilled to have gained such a cool friend.

At dinner time, it was absolute joy. Vicky had prepared her famous spaghetti, Bolognese style. Vicky was known for making a really mean Bolognese sauce. It was a recipe that was passed on to her by her favorite aunt, Ana. Even Mildred said that even though she didn't remember a thing from her past, she was willing to bet that she had never tasted anything like it.

On Saturdays, Vicky always allowed Amanda to sleep late. She also figured that the girls were way too excited to sleep early so she let the girls hang out a while longer. It was chilly out, so the girls decided to stay inside and watch movies.

There was nothing interesting for them to watch on television. After careful consideration, the girls decided to do the unthinkable. It was something that Vicky had always forbidden Amanda to do because Vicky knew that it would lead to permanent consequences: the girls decided to watch *The Exorcist*.

The Exorcist was a movie that came out in 1973 about a possessed twelve-year-old girl, and it scared the crap out of many.

Vicky and Eric had a collection of 1980s memorabilia that included posters, articles of clothes, candy, music, and movies from the '80s. Even though this movie came out in the early 1970's, Eric had included it in their collection. Vicky never wanted Amanda to watch it because she was afraid that Amanda would never be able to sleep alone again. Even grown men had a hard time sleeping alone after watching this movie. Amanda would never watch it alone, but she figured it would be okay since she had company.

Mildred went along with anything Amanda said. The tables were definitely turned. Little Amanda was now running the show. Mildred had pulled out the leader in her.

Because Vicky would never allow the girls to watch this movie, the girls snuck into Vicky's bedroom while Vicky was in the shower and Eric was playing with Junior downstairs. They went over to where Vicky and Eric kept their 1980's treasures and smuggled the movie out. Amanda did tell her mother that they were going to be up all night watching movies, but she didn't mention what movies they were.

After putting on their PJs and getting the perfect movie night mood on, they began to watch the movie. At first, the movie seemed to drag and was borderline boring. Amanda did not see what the big deal was at all. At one point, Mildred even suggested to change the movie, but then it happened: when Regan, the girl in the movie, was being tested to see if she had any psychological issues, a demon possessed her. It was so scary that both Amanda and Mildred let out a horrific scream.

"Aaaaahhh!"

With her heart coming out of her chest, Mildred said, "Oh my god, Mandy! That is the scariest thing I've ever seen in my life! I think."

"I know, me too!" said Amanda.

"Put it again!" said Mildred.

Amanda put the scene again. Again, they both screamed at the top of their lungs, "Aaaaaaahhh!"

"Holy crap! It's even scarier the second time around!" said Mildred.

"I know!"

"Put it again! Put it again!" insisted Mildred. She just couldn't get enough of it.

"Oh heck no, Milly! As a matter of fact, I'm turning this crap off! I should have listened to my mother. I doubt I'll be able to sleep now."

"Come on, what are you afraid of?" said Mildred.

"Hello? Spirits. Satan! You know, scary supernatural stuff like that."

"Don't be silly, Mandy. That stuff's not real."

"Girl, you have forgotten what real is. Let's just go to sleep."

Amanda took the movie out and turned off the television. Then they each went to their own beds. They were too scared to have the lights off completely so they used a night light that Amanda kept in her room. Both girls were lying on their backs just staring at the ceiling.

In the dead silence, Mildred said, "Mandy?"

"Yeah?"

"What was I like before the accident?"

"Well, you haven't changed much really."

"What did you like most about me? What made you choose me as a friend?"

Amanda did not know what to say. She remembered to stay positive and speak only good things to build Mildred up.

"You are the coolest! You are nice, friendly, and everybody loves you. There is nothing you wouldn't do for your friends and I love that about you. Besides, you're like the sister I wish I had."

"Really?"

"Yeah, really. Now can we please try to sleep?"

Mildred giggled a bit. "Okay."

It became very quiet. Everyone else was already asleep and they could hear a pin drop. As they lay on their beds in the dead silence, out came an undeniable sound.

Amanda farted really, really loud.

"What the heck was that, Amanda? Did you just fart?" said Mildred in shock.

"Um, no," said Amanda.

"Yeah right, Mandy! If it wasn't you, then who was it?"

"That must have been the spirits. You see, I told you they were real!" said Amanda, trying to be funny.

Mildred was laughing so hard that she almost peed on herself.

"You are so funny!" said Mildred.

"I know," said Amanda with a big grin on her face.

After gaining composure, Mildred decided to play the question game.

"What do you think is scarier, a strange man standing in front of your bed in the middle of the night or a strange woman?"

"Oh my god, Milly, a woman of course!"

"Why is that?" asked Mildred.

"Well, chances are that a man just wants to rape you or something like that, but at least you still have a shot at living. On the other hand, what the heck would a strange woman want in the middle of the night if not to kill you?"

"That's true. Okay, so how about this; a strange woman or a strange child?"

"Good Lord, Mildred! What is in that head of yours? Did the doctors leave some rocks in there?"

"Just tell me!"

After sighing, Amanda said, "I think a child is definitely creepier. A child can only mean one thing and that's ghost!"

Mildred continued, "Okay, what about this; a child or a midget?"

"You know what, Mildred? You need to shut up. Now you're just being ridiculous! Why the hell would a strange midget be in my room, standing beside my bed, in the middle of the night? Just go to sleep, we go to church tomorrow."

"Church? You guys go to church?"

"Yes, we go to church. Don't worry, it's only for an hour, then we all go out to eat. It's my favorite part."

"Okay then, goodnight, Mandy, and thanks for having me here."

"Sure thing! You're my best friend so why wouldn't I? Goodnight."

Amanda turned into a fetal position, closed her eyes, and had a big grin on her face. She was genuinely happy about how things were unfolding before her. There were moments where she truly believed that she and Mildred had been friends for a long time. They really did hit it off.

CHAPTER 11

∙∙

Praise the Lord!

*I*t was a beautiful Sunday morning and the Muses were ready to go to church. Just a few weeks after arriving in Colorado, they found a church nearby called Grace Community Church. The Muses were immediately drawn to it because it was small and cozy, and the members were very humble people. Unlike many churches, their main focus was the message of God's unconditional love and grace. Other churches the Muses had gone to in the past had a tendency to focus on sin, condemnation, and what people should be or should not be doing. Also, the services would last for hours at a time. In Grace Community Church, the pastor managed to preach a meaningful message in only thirty minutes.

Best of all, Grace Community Church was very active in the community. They always lend a helping hand, putting God's word into action. Their members were very involved in reaching out, not only to the community, but also overseas. Their mission was to reflect everything Jesus Christ stood for, which was love, mercy, compassion, and all that good stuff.

The church was not far from the Muses at all, yet the Muses always took the family van because they liked to go eat out after the service.

The Muses always made sure that they got to church early so that they had a chance to mingle with other church members. On arriving there, Mildred was pleased to see how friendly and welcoming the members were. This was something totally new to her.

The sermon that day was in reference to the scripture of 1 Corinthians 13:2 where it says, "If I have the gift of prophecy, and know all mysteries and all knowledge; and if I have all faith, so as to remove mountains, but do not have love, I am nothing."

The pastor's main focus was to make people aware that even if they know the Bible from beginning to end and go to church every Sunday, but did not have love for others, then it means nothing to God. The pastor did a great job in portraying this message of love and compassion for others and Mildred was very moved by it.

She didn't understand why, but it definitely hit home.

Toward the end of the service, the pastor asked for volunteers to help out with the distribution of food to the needy for Thanksgiving Day. This was only a few days away. Immediately, Amanda and Vicky thought about Bo. Amanda wanted to go back to the park and find out how Bo was doing after Coco's death and the incident with Mildred, but she was hesitant because she feared that Mildred would recognize him.

Both, Amanda and Vicky, realized that visiting Bo, especially for Thanksgiving, was inevitable. They knew that they were not going to be able to go around feeding the needy and skipping Bo. They were going to have to think of something.

After the service, the Muses went to their usual after-church lunch spot. It was at an Italian restaurant called Marcos' Pizza Pazza, which means 'Marcos' Crazy Pizza.' It was known for its famous New York City style pizza. Marcos' had a dine-in special where you could get a whole pizza pie for only ten dollars. Best of all, their pizza was amazing! Because the Muses came from the East Coast, it was like having a slice from home.

Everyone sat down and waited for their order. Because Marcos' always made their pizza fresh, the family always had to wait a while to get their order. This time waiting for their food gave the family a chance to bond.

Eric did not allow the use of cell phones or technology of any kind during this time. Without the technology, they were more likely to annoy each other. Realizing that kids nowadays are completely lost without technology, Eric initiated a conversation to set an example.

"So, Mildred, how do you like staying with us so far? I hope you feel comfortable enough that you can trust us."

"Yes, sir. So far it's been really nice being with you guys. I also appreciate that you have taken me in. I know that I live alone with my dad and all, but right now he's like a stranger to me. I know I would have felt very awkward alone with him."

"Yes, I understand. Just know that what your father is doing is honorable and morally responsible; you should be proud. Just let us know if there's anything we can do for you, okay?"

"Yes, sir. Thanks."

The waiter came to bring them their drinks. All the cups had lids on them.

Unsurprisingly, Junior did not waste any time removing the lid off of his cup to spin it. As he spun it, he began to stim by making loud humming noises. Sometimes, he got really loud. Feeling a little embarrassed, Vicky told him to stop and be quiet.

Mildred still had all of that love talk from church fresh in her mind. Feeling compassion towards Junior, Mildred took the lid off of her cup and began to spin it without any hesitation. She also made humming noises.

"Okay, now you two are just being silly. Behave yourselves," said Vicky.

"I don't mean to disrespect Mrs. V, but I don't think that he's able to relate to us or the world we live in. Maybe if we play the only way he understands, we can somehow relate to him; you know what I mean?"

Junior made very little eye contact with people and was often consumed in his own little world. The family couldn't help to notice that, for that brief moment, when Mildred was playing along with him, Junior was making eye contact and interacting with her.

"You know, babe, Mildred here might have a point," said Eric, "I have never seen Junior relate to anybody before."

Again, Mildred proceeded to spin her lid and make noises right along with him. She even invited Amanda to play along. In the beginning, Amanda was a little embarrassed, but then Mildred reminded her about the church sermon.

"Come on, Mandy. Didn't you get anything from today's sermon?" she said.

"What about?" said Amanda.

Mildred couldn't believe that Amanda was not at all moved by it.

"You know, love, caring, and all that. Did you not hear a word the pastor said?" said Mildred.

Amanda was happy to hear those words coming from Mildred. She giggled, "Look at you, little Miss Thang! You're all Mother Teresa-ish and compassionate now."

"Well, wasn't I compassionate before?"

"Umm, yeah, but I don't know. I'm just glad that you haven't changed," Amanda said realizing that she almost put her foot in her mouth.

Wanting to change the subject, Amanda immediately began to play along. Now the Muses had three children spinning lids on the table and making noise. Vicky and Eric became more comfortable with the idea and did not mind it at all.

They were thrilled to see that for the first time, Junior was interacting with others and having a real good time.

All that good time was interrupted when the pizza finally arrived. They said grace and dug in. It had been a very good day so far for the Muse family. In the end, both Vicky and Eric thanked Mildred for lightening things up.

When they were all done, they realized that there were three slices of pizza left. After meeting Bo, Vicky and Amanda could not get themselves to throw away any food. They both had Bo on their minds and wanted to take the slices of pizza to him. Even though they were both a little concerned that Mildred would remember him, the urge to feed him was greater than whatever would follow thereafter.

"Hey, Mildred, now that you are all fired up about today's sermon, do you mind going with Amanda and me to the park to give these leftover slices to the homeless?" said Vicky. "There's a homeless guy there that we bring food to sometimes. His name is Bo."

"Mom?" said Amanda concerned.

"It's okay, honey. It'll be fine," said Vicky.

"Sure thing, Mrs. V. I'd be happy to do so!" said Mildred.

"Great! We can all go and do this as a family. What do you say, Eric?"

"Sure, I don't see why not. Let's hurry up though because I want to see the game. The Broncos are playing the Patriots today and I do not want to miss that!"

"Oh, we'll be home by then. Promise," said Vicky.

Amanda was feeling uneasy about going to meet Bo with Mildred. At this point, she needed to trust that all was going to be fine. The Muses packed up and went to Lakewood Park.

Once there, Vicky asked Mildred, "So Mildred, is anything familiar to you?"

"No, ma'am, not at all," Mildred said to Amanda's relief.

Even though she did not remember a thing, Amanda was still concerned about Mildred meeting Bo. She worried that Bo might spill the beans himself by apologizing or saying something to Mildred that would indicate that he was guilty. Regardless, there was nothing they could do at that point. They were already in the park and there was no turning back.

As they approached Bo's tent, Amanda told the family that she'd walk ahead just to make sure that Bo was there and that they were not going to disturb him or anything like that. The family didn't make anything of it and Amanda went to get to him first.

Amanda made it to the tent first and found Bo reading the newspaper.

In a rushed whisper she said, "Bo, no time to explain, just know that Mildred doesn't remember a thing. Please, just play along."

"Huh?" said Bo.

"Shhhh! Just don't say anything! I'll explain later."

The Muses made it to Bo's tent shortly after. Bo came out and was not sure of what to expect. Here was Amanda's entire family coming over with a box of pizza and Mildred, the bully he assaulted a few days ago, by their side.

"Hey, Bo," said Vicky.

"Hey," said Bo, "What are you guyth doing here?"

"Oh, we just had pizza with the family and thought that you might like some," said Vicky.

"Food ith alwayth welcomed here. Lookth like you have your entire family with you today, ma'am."

"Yes, I do. This is my husband, Eric, my son Eric Jr., and Amanda's friend, Mildred. She's staying with us for a little while."

Bo didn't know what to say.

After a few seconds, he finally said, "Wow, thtaying with you, eh?"

"Yup," said Amanda. "She's staying with us because a rock fell on her head and now she has anemia. We are very happy to have her staying with us though."

"It's amnesia, silly. I have amnesia," said Mildred giggling.

Bo was surprised to hear that Mildred had amnesia. Still, he felt relieved.

"Well, it lookth like you've got quite a bump there, young lady," he said.

"Yes, I do. A rock fell on my head right in this park."

Amanda sighed quietly in relief as she realized that Mildred had no idea who Bo was.

"She'll be good in no time," said Eric.

Handing Bo the box of leftover pizza, Vicky said, "Well, Bo, I see you're a little busy reading your paper. We're going to head home. We don't want to take much of your time. We just wanted to bring over some food."

"Oh, it'th no bother at all, ma'am. I wath jutht reading thith paper to zee if there'th any work for me out there. I really want to try and leave thith plathe. It jutht ithn't the thame here without Coco and it ith that time to do thomething, you know?"

"Oh, Bo, that is wonderful!" said Vicky, "I wish you the best of luck."

"Thank you, ma'am. It'th really hard though. Theemth like nobody ith willing to give a homeleth perthon a break. I do appreciate you taking the time to bring thith to me though. It really meanth a lot. May God bleth you and your beautiful family."

"What kind of work are you looking for, my friend?" said Eric.

"Zir, I am willing to do anything. I'm a hard worker and have great attention to detail. It'th hard though. Without a thet of fresh clotheth and a plathe to shower, the oddth of me getting a job ith zero. My thkills mean nothing if I'm dirty and thmelly. Nobody will hire me if I'm dirty."

"You know what, man? Let me do some talking where I work. I'm not making any promises, but I give you my word that I'll keep you in mind. We just might have something for you okay, brother?"

"Oh, honey, that's wonderful!" said Vicky with excitement.

"Thank you zo much, zir, and thank you for thith meal. God bleth you!"

"Okay man, don't mention it," said Eric.

The Muses said goodbye to Bo and left the park with a sense of accomplishment. Mildred was very moved by Eric's gesture. She couldn't help thinking that anybody, including herself, could be one misfortune away from being homeless, hungry, and cold; and with no one to lend a hand. She remembered that the church was providing meals for Thanksgiving.

She turned to Vicky. "Mrs. V, maybe we should invite Bo to church for Thanksgiving."

"Oh dear, I can't believe we forgot to mention that to him!"

"We can go back and tell him, Mom," said Amanda.

"Why don't we do something better and invite him over for dinner," said Eric.

"Eric, what are you saying?" said a surprised Vicky.

"Well," he continued, "I've been thinking that since we need someone to help us out at work, maybe we can hire this guy and give him a chance."

"Oh my god, Eric, that'll be awesome!" said Vicky.

"We have some properties that need some repairs to prepare them for viewing. Some painting, repairing, and cleaning is always needed. It's been really hard to find somebody though. Seems like no one is willing to do the dirty work. With this guy, we can help each other out. He can shower and sleep in one of these houses until they are sold. He'll have a chance to save money and then he can move to his own place. It's perfect!"

"It *is* perfect, Dad!" said Amanda, "I'll go tell him now! Come on, Mildred, let's go tell him!"

"Oh no, you're not, young lady! You are going to have to wait. There are a couple of things that I need to do first."

"When will you know, Dad?"

"Tomorrow I will talk to the right people and see what they say."

"Okay, but don't forget!"

"I won't."

Everyone was thrilled, especially the girls. They also had to get ready for school the next day. It would be the first day of school for the new Mildred. Amanda felt butterflies in her stomach every time she thought about it. She couldn't wait to introduce Mildred to her new friends.

It had only been two days since Mildred joined the Muses, but she had already learned and changed so much. The fear of anything or anyone triggering some memory back to Mildred was always in the back of Amanda's mind. Everything was going as planned so far, so Amanda decided to relax a little and just trust.

At bedtime, the girls had one of their late-night talks; mainly a lot of question asking from Mildred. Mildred wanted to know how things were at school, how many friends did she have, and how were the teachers. Amanda kept it short and sweet. She reminded Mildred that their teachers were very nice and that their friends were Lucinda, Sky, and Daniel. Amanda asked Mildred again if she remembered any of them, but she didn't. Then Amanda asked Mildred if she remembered Liz at all, but Mildred was completely blanked out.

Amanda ended the conversation by telling Mildred that it was best for Mildred to wait till she got to school to know more. Mildred agreed and they went to sleep.

CHAPTER 12

Back to School

*I*t was a beautiful Monday morning when the new Mildred returned to school. Amanda felt refreshed when she saw familiar faces. Mildred saw a bunch of kids she did not know, but who knew her. She was so glad to have her 'bestie,' Amanda, right beside her at all times. All the other kids were pleasantly surprised to see the two together. They remembered to not say anything and play along. They were looking forward to a nice, bully-free environment at school.

Amanda went to her locker as usual. Once there, Mildred met Lucinda. Mildred had no recollection of Lucinda whatsoever and Lucinda was very amused by it.

They exchanged a couple of words as if they were meeting each other for the first time. Then both Amanda and Lucinda walked Mildred to her locker.

As the three 'amigas' were approaching Mildred's locker, they saw Liz who was right there getting ready for class. Liz felt a little awkward when she saw her buddy so chummy with her new friends. These were the same people Mildred had hated so much. Liz did not want to talk too much in case Mildred remembered her and made good on her promise to beat her up. Liz decided to play it by ear and wait to see Mildred's reaction.

When the girls got to Mildred's locker, Liz was relieved to see no reaction from Mildred.

Liz said, "Hey, Mildred, how are you feeling?"

"I'm good I guess. And you are?" said Mildred.

"I'm Liz, your friend, remember me?"

"I'm sorry, but I don't. I barely remember Mandy whom I hear is my best friend."

Liz could not believe what she was hearing. Since when have Mildred and Amanda been best friends? This was ludicrous! Desperate to resume her friendship with Mildred and regain their rule over the school, Liz attempted to spill the beans and let Mildred know who was who in this game.

Liz said, "Well, in reality, you're *my* best friend. You have been since we began coming to this school. As a matter of fact, we hate these girls. They think they are all that and I suggest that we make their lives miserable just like they have done to us for so long."

Mildred was stunned and confused with all of the negativity coming out of Liz's mouth. Amanda and Lucinda looked at each other in wonder.

"What? What are you talking about?" said Mildred confused.

"Don't listen to her, Mildred," said Lucinda, "She's a loser who has no friends. Nobody likes her. Now she wants to make you believe that you're her friend."

"That is so not true, Mildred! They're the ones who-"

"You know what, Mildred?" said Amanda. "Let's just ask around. The whole school would agree that Liz has no friends because she's mean to everybody."

Liz quickly realized that she was fighting a losing battle. She really didn't have many friends. Liz had spent all year mistreating people. Now she was on her own without her bodyguard.

As Mildred got ready for class, she dismissed everything that Liz had said.

She turned to Liz. "I don't know who you or any of you guys are. The only thing I know right now is that Amanda was the only person that went to see me at the hospital and that her family has been nothing but good to me. If you are such a good friend, then where have you been all this time? You didn't even go see me when I was in the hospital!"

"Mildred, I-"

"You know what? Let's just go to class," said Mildred, not wanting to hear another word.

She did not understand what was going on, but did not care to know either. Her life, after leaving the hospital, had been a bliss. She was not even sure if she wanted to remember her past.

Mildred, Amanda, and Lucinda headed to class. As they walked and distanced themselves from Liz, Lucinda discreetly turned around and stuck her tongue out at Liz. Even though Liz was furious, she couldn't help but admit that this was probably an opportunity for a fresh new start for her too; a start without fear.

There were times where Liz had also been a victim of Mildred's bullying. Maybe not in an obvious way, but perhaps in a way that was much worse. Liz had been denied the privilege of being herself. Liz was not picked on as long as she did everything Mildred told her to do. Sometimes Liz found herself doing things that were uncomfortable for her, but she was too afraid to stand up to Mildred.

Frankly, Liz was beginning to get tired of always complying with Mildred's reign of terror. Maybe there was something good about this plan after all. Maybe there was a light at the end of the tunnel. Liz could finally be free to be herself.

There were other girls she always wanted to be friends with, but Mildred would aggressively and jealously convince her not to. Liz didn't even feel free to admit she liked a boy or anything because she was afraid of Mildred's possessiveness. Liz decided that it was time to be herself and make new friends.

There was a girl named Sharon White, who was not only Liz's neighbor but a friend of the Lombardi family as well. They were both the same age and Sharon also attended Lakewood Junior High. Sharon always tried to befriend Liz, but eventually gave up because Liz would never give her the time of day. It was not because Liz didn't like her—in fact, Liz always thought that Sharon was cool—but Liz was always afraid of Mildred. Now that Mildred had amnesia and had chosen a new group of friends, Liz could finally choose who to hang out with. Liz hoped that Sharon would still be interested in being friends.

The first period biology class went great. Everyone was glad to have the new Mildred in class. They all got a kick out of seeing the nicer version of her. To everyone's surprise, she actually came across as very pleasant. Even Mr. Erickson was pleasantly surprised. Mrs. Dotson had briefly mentioned the plan to all of Mildred's teachers and they unanimously concluded that if it would bring peace to the classroom, then it was all worth it.

The second period rolled around and Lucinda departed to another class while Amanda and Mildred went to their math class. That was where Mildred met Daniel.

Not knowing what to do or say, Daniel started off by saying, "Hey, girl, what's going on?"

There was a certain quirkiness to Daniel that made everything he said sound funny and welcoming. There was something inviting about his aura that made everyone feel comfortable around him, even if it was the first time you had ever met him.

This made Mildred feel very comfortable with him. She responded, "Nothing, bro, what's up with you?"

Amanda found this to be hilarious because this was the first time that the new Mildred had ever met Daniel. It was just refreshing to see Mildred with, not only a sense of humor, but open to meeting new people and being friendly.

Amanda had already spoken to Mildred about Daniel before class. Mildred knew right away that she was talking to the man himself.

She confirmed it by saying, "You must be Daniel. Mandy has told me a lot about you."

"Yup, that is I. And you must be bump-on-the-head, don't-remember-a- thing Mildred? Just kidding. Nice to see you again. How's that knot on your head? Looks pretty painful."

"It's good. It's not as bad as it looks."

"Everyone, have a seat," said Mrs. Clancy, "Mildred Riley, welcome back. I'm Mrs. Clancy, your math teacher. Please let me know if you need anything, anything at all. Okay, dear?"

"Yes, ma'am. I will. Thanks."

'Yes, ma'am' and 'thanks' coming from Mildred Riley? Mrs. Clancy could not believe her ears. She was also surprised by the changes.

"How's Mr. Riley?" asked Mrs. Clancy.

"He's good, I guess," said Mildred.

"You guess? What do you mean you guess?"

"Well, he'll be away for ninety days and I haven't spoken to him. He's in a program where they don't allow calls or contact with anybody for the first three weeks."

Mrs. Clancy did not want to pry, so she left it alone. She was not sure what program Mildred was talking about, but she had an idea. Mildred's life at home was no secret. Everyone knew that she was being raised by a single dad and that Joe took it pretty hard when Mildred's mother left him. This was why the staff felt a little sorry for Mildred and sometimes let her get away with some things.

"Oh, I'm so happy for him!" said Mrs. Clancy.

"Yeah, me too. I'm staying with my friend Amanda for now."

Mrs. Clancy was ever so pleased to hear Mildred speak that way. Mildred seemed happy, content, and even more mature. Mildred was never open about her personal life. She was too ashamed of it. Now she seemed to be embracing it, which was refreshing on all levels.

"Well, I'm very happy for you and your dad. Okay then, everyone, put everything away; I am giving you a pop quiz."

"A pop quiz? Where did this come from, Mrs. Clancy?" said Amanda concerned.

"Well, if it's a pop quiz, then I guess it popped out of nowhere, Miss Amanda Muse," said Mrs. Clancy sarcastically.

"Mrs. Clancy, Mildred here has just popped her head! Don't you think that there's been enough popping lately? Do we really need more popping? Can't you have some compassion? I mean, she probably can't even remember what two plus two is!" said Amanda trying to negotiate an extension on the quiz.

"You know, Amanda, you may have a point. Let's allow Mildred to warm up a little bit for now," said Mrs. Clancy.

Mrs. Clancy then turned her attention over to the rest of the class and said, "You guys are not off the hook just yet. Study tonight and every night this week because you are going to be tested one of these days and I'm not going to tell you when."

The class was grateful and even applauded Amanda for getting them an extension on the quiz, including Liz who was sitting quietly in the back of the classroom.

For the first time in a long time, math class went smoothly. Everyone was on their best behavior. It seemed that they all had something to prove. They all wanted to set the tone for Mildred on how a perfect school day should be.

At lunchtime, Amanda, Lucinda, Daniel, and Sky sat together as always, only this time, they added Mildred to their little clique. Mildred was introduced to Sky and the group was complete. They noticed Liz joining Sharon and her little crew. It seemed like everything was falling right into place.

Mildred asked, "What's up with that Liz chick?"

"Don't know, she has issues," said Lucinda.

"So Mildred, how do you like the school and us so far?" said Sky.

"All is great except for this morning. That Liz chick freaked me out."

"Yeah, Liz can do that. But who cares about her, she's doing fine with her friends," said Sky.

"Yeah, I guess. Hey, Daniel, how come you don't hang out with the boys?" said Mildred.

"I'm not manly enough for them," said Daniel chuckling.

"What do you mean you're not manly enough?" asked Mildred.

"Relax, dudette. I just rather hang out with chicks that's all."

"Well, I think it's nice that you are manly enough to admit that," said Sky.

"Mildred, just so you know, Daniel does not let anything bother him," added Amanda.

"So, how did you guys spend the weekend? It must be awkward for you having to stay at Mandy's house," Daniel said to Mildred.

"You know what, Daniel? Mandy and I must really be close friends because I did not feel awkward at all. Her family is really nice and believe me, Amanda made sure that we got comfortable right away."

"What do you mean?" said Lucinda.

"Well, while we were having a late-night talk, she farted!"

"No way! Not little Miss Amanda Muse!" said Daniel in shock.

"Yes way! Really loud too!"

"Stop exaggerating, Mildred," said Amanda.

"Exaggerating? Amanda, you were close to launching and taking off like a rocket with that fart!"

They were all laughing.

Mildred continued, "Then, she had the audacity to blame the spirits!"

"Spirits? What spirits?" said Sky.

"It's a long story. We were talking about a whole bunch of scary stuff," said Amanda.

Then Lucinda turned to Mildred and said, "Oh, and you didn't come up with a name of choice to tease her with for farting?"

Lucinda said this impulsively, remembering how Mildred used to call her "Gassy Lucy." All of a sudden, it was like a record that was playing, scratched, and stopped abruptly. Everything went silent.

"No. Why would I do that? I mean, everybody farts," said Mildred.

"Wow," said Lucinda in amazement, "How interesting."

"Okay, Lucinda, now *you're* being all weird," said Mildred confused. She dismissed Lucinda's remark altogether.

Amanda, concerned that Mildred might remember "Gassy Lucy," said, "Can we please stop talking about our intestinal outbursts, please? For God's sake, we're eating!"

"Agreed!" said Daniel.

Mildred went on explaining how she and the Muses spent the rest of their weekend. She told her new friends about church and Bo. She even invited them to join the Muses as they volunteer to feed the homeless for Thanksgiving. They were all amazed to see Mildred so eager to help others. They went along with her to the point that Mildred truly believed that this was who she was and had always been.

Not too long into their lunch break, the gang had completely forgotten how wicked Mildred was before the accident. They embraced her and started to enjoy her company. The feeling was mutual. Mildred also appreciated her new friends at school.

The rest of the week went on perfectly. Mildred grew closer and closer to her new friends and enjoyed every minute with them. At home, Amanda and Mildred started to see each other more like sisters. Mildred helped out mostly with Junior. Both Junior and Mildred had developed a very special connection that Amanda's parents very much appreciated.

Mildred spent countless hours during the week playing with Junior. Mildred would spin things with him and then suggest that they'd take turns in playing something she liked, like basketball. For the first time, Junior was sympathetic toward others. He was even willing to leap out of his world and join someone else's, even if for a brief moment. This was huge! The Muses were never able to get Junior to do anything that did not involve spinning objects.

The family started to notice how Junior's ability to relate to others had improved. He was making more eye contact with people and relating to them. This was something he always struggled with in the past.

Eric and Vicky were amazed, and their hearts were filled with joy as they watched their son shoot hoops with Mildred and Amanda. Every day, Vicky became more convinced that bringing Mildred to stay with them was a great idea. She saw the good hand of karma coming right back to them. When the Muses offered to help, they did it without expecting anything in return. Yet they found themselves receiving the benefits of doing a good deed. It truly was a great time!

CHAPTER 13

••

Thanksgiving Eve

*T*he time came to make preparations for Thanksgiving Day. The Muses had been looking forward to this for a couple of weeks. They decided to invite Bo, not only to help with the distribution of the food, but to join them for dinner at their home.

It was Thanksgiving Eve, and volunteers from Grace Community Church had gathered all of the food that was donated to them by their church members. The volunteers were to sort out all of the food in boxes, assuring that each box got a complete traditional Thanksgiving meal.

All of the boxes needed to include: a turkey, cranberry sauce, canned yams, corn, stuffing, marshmallows, and an apple cider. After filling up the boxes, the volunteers were instructed to deliver them to known low-income families. The remaining boxes were to be stored at the church for any family in need to pick up.

All of the volunteers, including the Muses, were very happy to help. There is just something amazing that happens to the soul when one chooses to give. There's greatness when you decide to be the doctor and not the patient.

That day, Grace Community Church successfully delivered twenty-eight boxes of food to needy families. Another twelve boxes were picked up at the church.

In total, Grace Community Church distributed forty boxes filled with a complete Thanksgiving meal to needy families in the community.

Bo never showed up to help. He was too embarrassed to show up smelly and unclean. Vicky and Amanda did not forget about him though. Their plan was to finish volunteering for the church, go home to prepare for their own Thanksgiving, stop at the local thrift shop to pick up some clothes for Bo, and then go over to see him. Then they could formally invite Bo to dine with them on Thanksgiving Day.

After a long day of giving, the Muses went home to prepare for their own Thanksgiving. Vicky always liked to season her turkey a day or two before Thanksgiving to make sure that all of the flavors locked in. The rest of the family was responsible for helping clean the house.

Amanda and Mildred finished their chores right away. They asked Vicky if they could go clothes shopping for Bo. Eric immediately volunteered to take them. Eric hated shopping and cleaning, but out of the two, shopping was the lesser of the two evils. He would much rather shop than clean. So off they went to a thrift shop that was only a couple of blocks away.

They all knew what they wanted to get Bo. They wanted to get him a set of the basic attire which consisted of: a pair of pants, at least two shirts, one pair of shoes, some socks and underwear.

The only problem was finding plus sizes for Bo. For a homeless person, Bo was a pretty big guy, not only in height, but in weight as well.

Bo was always lucky to have people give him food. Unfortunately, he always got fast food. One particular guy, a regular at Lakewood Park, worked in a bagel-and-donut shop that prided themselves on making and selling fresh bagels and donuts every day. Every night at closing time, the shop would throw away dozens of leftover bagels and donuts to maintain their reputation of having fresh food every day. Unbeknownst to the store manager, this one employee would come back after everybody was gone, to get the leftover bagels and donuts. He would then distribute them to the homeless people at Lakewood Park.

One day, the store manager installed surveillance cameras all around the store for security reasons. The cameras recorded all after-hour activities and sadly for this employee, he was caught taking the leftover food and was fired immediately.

When he asked what the big deal was, since the food was being thrown in the trash anyway, he was told that it was not good for business. The employer felt that if he allowed this, customers would not buy in his store but rather wait till the 'trash' was taken out to get free food. Go figure.

The homeless people in Lakewood Park stopped getting their bagels and donuts which had kept them plump for a long time. They never heard from this guy again and often wondered whatever happened to him.

After walking up and down the aisles of the thrift store for about fifteen minutes, Eric finally decided to ask one of the ladies working there, where he could find the plus sizes for men. The lady was very helpful and politely directed him to the plus sizes for men.

The good thing about plus size clothes is that because they are not as popular, they are often less expensive, if they aren't already on sale. Eric was able to buy Bo two buttoned shirts and three T-shirts for everyday use. He also got him one pair of semi-formal pants, two pairs of jeans, and a pair of black sneakers that he could easily use as dressy shoes. It all came out to a grand total of $37.00.

The girls were super excited. They couldn't wait to see Bo in his new clothes; showered, clean, and shaved. Also, they couldn't wait to see Bo with a new hairdo.

Bo did not comb or wash his hair very often and it looked very scruffy. They expressed their excitement to Eric. It had not occurred to him that Bo was going to need a haircut. Eric quickly concluded that once Bo showered in the vacant house that he was to stay in temporarily, Vicky could give Bo a haircut.

Junior was very restless as a child, and Vicky learned how to cut hair just to be able to give Junior his haircuts. Sometimes it would take her two days to finish cutting his hair. She used the clippers to trim his hair one day, and leave the outline for the following day. Throughout the years, Vicky became very good at it. Cutting Bo's hair was not going to be a problem for her at all.

Next, they went to the local department store. There, they picked up a bag of extra-large underwear and a bag of socks. Then they went back home and proudly waltzed through the door with all of their shopping bags. Surprisingly, this shopping trip had given Eric a lot of pleasure as well as a sense of pride and worth.

At first, he was just doing it to go along with the family's wishes, but he actually enjoyed it to his own surprise.

In a state of euphoria, Eric showed Vicky everything he bought. He told her that he was going to take Bo to one of the vacant houses and allow Bo to shower there. Then she could cut his hair. He also said that he was going to talk to his boss immediately to try and get Bo a job doing handyman work on the houses that needed to be repaired in order to be sold. Vicky was a sucker for this kind of stuff.

She looked at her man and was ever so proud. She had no trouble expressing how much she respected him, which gave Eric even more fuel. If you want to bring out the best in a man, all you need to do is show him respect and praise him for the little things, even if it's just because he carried a bag of groceries.

"You know what, babe?" Eric said with his eyes wide open, "Bo can probably do some repairs in this old house we're trying to fix and put on the market. He can live there rent free while he works on it. It would give him a chance to save money so he can later rent his own place."

"Oh, honey, that's an excellent idea! I'm sure that that will make him very happy," said Vicky.

Eric did not waste any time. He immediately called his boss and told him about Bo. His boss was not too thrilled with the idea, but Eric managed to convince him by taking full responsibility if anything should go wrong. Eric's boss reluctantly agreed under those conditions.

Eric realized that he was taking a chance on this stranger, but there was something about Bo that inspired trust.

After everyone was done with their chores, they all began to prepare for dinner. As always, Vicky cooked, the kids set the table, and Eric prepared the beverages. As everyone took part in their daily routine, Mildred admired the way the family worked together. Although she was happy to be with the Muses, she did feel a little envious because her family setting was not nearly as structured. She also felt a little scared of what would happen when she went back home with her dad. The Muses were a picture-perfect family, or at least that's how they seemed to Mildred.

As everyone sat down to have dinner, they noticed that Mildred became quiet and distant.

In efforts to break the ice, Vicky turned to Mildred and said, "Mildred, honey, is everything okay?"

"Yes, ma'am. Why do you ask?"

"Well, you seem a bit quiet."

"Well, I was thinking that I can probably call my father next week; you know, see how he's doing."

"Of course, dear! As soon as we are able to call him, we will. I want to know how he's doing myself."

"I would also like to know more about my mom's whereabouts if that's okay."

Vicky looked around at the family wondering if she should say anything about Mildred's mother being in jail. She wasn't sure if Joe had mentioned anything to her about it. Ultimately, Vicky decided that the best thing was not to get involved. After all, it was not her place to have that discussion with her. Besides, Vicky did not know exactly what happened to Mildred's mother and how she ended up in jail.

"I'm sure that when you speak to your father, you can ask him yourself," said Vicky.

"Yeah, okay. I can do that," said Mildred.

Once that was settled, the family continued with their dinner. Then, the topic of Bo came up and it lifted everyone's spirits including

Mildred's. Everyone was looking forward to having Bo over for Thanksgiving and everyone had their own personal reasons why.

After dinner, everyone cleaned up. Vicky gathered all of the leftovers and put them in a Tupperware to take to Bo. This time, only the girls in the family went to see Bo. Eric stayed home with Junior and relaxed a bit. A day of shopping can really take a toll on a man.

While they were walking toward the park, all three ladies started thinking. They began to realize just how lucky they were. It was about 37°F outside and very windy, which made the temperature feel even lower. Even though they felt cold, at least they knew that they had a warm home to go back to. They couldn't even imagine what it would be like to sleep on a hard floor, hungry and cold in even worse weather.

They began to walk a little faster in a vain effort to beat the chill. When they got to Bo's camp, they were happy to see that the homeless people there had their own personal campfire going. The fire kept them from freezing to death. Bo noticed the ladies approaching him and was very happy to see them.

"Hello, my ladieth. How are you all doing thith evening?" he said.

"Oh, Bo, it is so cold out here, how do you do it?" asked Vicky.

"You get uthed to it. And how are you my lady?" he said to Mildred, "How'th that old bump on your head?"

"It's okay. I feel it less every day. The stitches are coming out after Thanksgiving."

"I am zo glad to hear that," said Bo.

"We wanted to bring you some food," said Amanda trying to change the subject.

"Little lady, I'm alwayth happy when you bring me food, but tonight I am ethpecially grateful."

"And why is that Bo?" said Vicky.

"Well, we had a guy who uthed to bring uth bagelth and donutth, but he hath not been around, and with thith cold weather, other people don't come around as often. I haven't had a bite to eat all day."

Even though Amanda and Vicky were very sorry to hear that, Mildred literally felt her heart tighten. She didn't say much, however, she definitely felt a calling.

She looked at all of the other homeless people there and wondered about what was going on with them. It broke her heart to see them hungry and cold. She wondered what happened to them that they ended up in this situation.

For a brief moment, she felt somewhat angry that they had gotten themselves into this mess. Then she quickly realized that this could have easily been her. If it weren't for people like Vicky and her family, who knew where she would have ended up? If her father had not gone into rehab, he would have been unemployed and unable to provide. Mildred was too young to work, so in reality, the Riley's were not too far from being homeless themselves.

"Bo, we can't stay here for long," said Vicky. "We just wanted to bring you some food and to formally invite you to have Thanksgiving dinner with us tomorrow at our home."

Bo looked at them in disbelief. When he realized that Vicky was serious, he fell to his knees and began to cry. It became a little awkward for everybody because they all understood why he was so emotional and humbled. They didn't even have to ask. His actions spoke sermons. It had probably been years since Bo had a decent meal anywhere. He had most likely forgotten what that was like. Vicky squatted down to his level and lifted his head.

She said, "It's okay, Bo, we know."

"Ma'am, I am zo dirty and I don't know where to-"

"I said it's okay, Bo, we've got this. Tomorrow, my husband Eric will pick you up around two o'clock and he'll take care of you, okay? He's already talked to his boss and got you a job and a place to stay until you earn enough money to move out."

"Oh, God bleth you, ma'am! God bleth you and your family!" Bo said sniffing and wiping away his tears.

"God has already blessed us, Bo," said Vicky, "We're just trying to pass some of it on, that's all."

With that, the ladies said their goodbyes and went home. On the way back, Mildred turned to Vicky and said, "Mrs. V, you're an angel."

Surprised, Vicky replied, "I hardly think so, Mildred. Believe me, I'm no angel."

"Yeah, believe her, she's no angel," said Amanda, "She can yell and beat you silly. Isn't that right, Mom?"

"That's right, Amanda!" said Vicky, "That, my lady, is called discipline and caring for your family."

"Yeah, okay," said Amanda, "Care for us a little less, will ya?"

"What I mean is," Vicky continued, "I have my flaws like everybody else and I'm not perfect. I just try and help whenever I can. It keeps me sane. You see, girls, if you are able to help somebody out but choose not to, then that decision will make you a bitter and miserable person, and that is a very sad place to be."

The girls did not have much to say. They were just trying to digest and hang on every word that Vicky was saying. They were beginning to see for themselves that she was right. All these things that they were doing in efforts to help other people had made them feel more content, and the more they did, the better they felt and the more they wanted to keep doing. This was something that Amanda never imagined would make her so happy, let alone Mildred.

Even though Mildred did not remember her past, one thing was absolutely clear: at that moment she was happy. Although she would only be with the Muses temporarily, she was happy to know that she had friends and people who truly cared about her. She may not have had the ideal family setting at home, but her father was trying his best to make it work and it was up to her how she viewed her situation. Mildred had the option to complain and be miserable or she could be grateful that she was not in a park, hungry and cold with nobody to talk to.

As they were walking, Mildred noticed an abandoned hula-hoop one block away from the house. It was very colorful.

She picked it up, and when Vicky asked her why she wanted the dirty old thing, Mildred simply said, "It's for Junior. I'm sure he'd love to spin this."

Vicky could not argue with her. Mildred seemed to understand Junior more than his own mother. Vicky was grateful for Mildred at that moment more than ever. Vicky knew that she would have never thought of bringing an old hula-hoop home for her son. She was always so busy trying to get Junior to act 'normal' that she never considered what was 'normal' to him. Through Mildred's example, Vicky learned to meet her son halfway.

Sure enough, when they got home, Mildred showed Junior the hula-hoop and he was ecstatic. He got so excited that you could almost see his eyes glow.

"Look, Junior, we can spin this baby up!" said Mildred adding more fuel to his excitement.

He put his hands together and began to jump up and down with enthusiasm.

"Ooooh, let me, let me!" he said.

"Ah, ah, aaah. You need to say, 'Thank you, Mildred' and give me a hug and a kissy."

He ran toward her and gave her a big hug and a kiss. "Thank you, Mildred!"

This was incredible! The family had never seen Junior interact this much with a stranger in his entire life. For a long time, he was just a kid who needed special care. Now, here he was, with an actual friend who he could relate to.

Mildred and Junior wasted no time whatsoever. He began spinning the hula-hoop first. Mildred was also into it and she demanded her turn. Then Amanda joined in. All three kids were playing until the rest of the family settled, showered, and got ready for bed. They spent nearly an hour spinning the darn thing. Surprisingly, they found it to be quite fun.

When Vicky was done with getting everything ready for bedtime, she went to where the kids were playing. She had originally gone there to tell them that it was time for bed, but when she saw her kids playing and having fun, she had this incredible urge to thank Mildred, which she did. She couldn't even tell her why because there were too many reasons, but she thanked her anyway in hopes that someday, when Mildred has kids of her own, she'd understand.

"You know what would be really cool, Mrs. V?" said Mildred. "If we can get some glow-in-the-dark stickers or glow-in-the-dark paint for this hula-hoop so we can spin it in the dark!"

"Oh, wow! That would be nice!" said Vicky.

"Cool! Glow in the dark, so cool!" said Junior.

Looking at her son's enthusiasm, Vicky felt obliged to grant them their wishes.

"You know what, guys? On Friday, I'll see if I can find something to light that baby up, okay?" she said.

"Awesome, Mrs. V!" said Mildred, "Thank you so much!"

"No, Mildred, thank you. Now go take a shower so you girls can go to sleep. We have a big day tomorrow."

"Yes, Mrs. V, will do."

With that, everyone settled and went to bed. They were too exhausted to stick around and watch movies or even to have their late night talks. The minute their heads hit their pillows, they were instantly knocked out and did not wake up until the next morning.

CHAPTER 14

∙∙∙

Thanksgiving Day

Thanksgiving morning was absolutely gorgeous that year in Colorado. The sun was out bright and warm. Coloradans always say, "If you don't like the weather in Colorado, just wait five minutes." You can have freezing cold weather one minute and warm the next. You just never know in Colorado.

Everyone woke up zestful. They all felt that they had a purpose and a duty that day. Their hearts were filled with lots and lots of love, which made them feel happy. Vicky showed her love toward her family through her cooking; Eric wanted to make a new man out of Bo and was filled with love there; Mildred and Amanda were overwhelmed with sisterly love and were happy to spend such a special day with each other; and Junior was overwhelmed with love toward his family and hula-hoop.

Everyone was busy doing their own thing. Eric left early that morning to prepare the house that Bo would be working on. Vicky put on her favorite '80s playlist and got cooking to the tune of Miami Sound Machine's 'Conga' while the girls did their nails, worked on each other's hair, and picked out their outfits.

It was easier to fix Mildred up than it was Amanda. Mildred had straight hair and you really could not do much with it. Amanda, on the other hand, had curly and thick hair. Mildred had no idea what to do with it. In the end, Mildred decided that leaving Amanda's hair loose was best. Amanda begged to differ.

"Mildred!" complained Amanda as she looked at herself in the mirror, "I look like Mufasa!"

"Who's Mufasa?" said Mildred.

"Mufasa, the Lion King!"

"You do not!" said Mildred, understanding the reference.

"I do too! You look like Beauty while I look like the Beast! Think of something else, Milly, and do it fast!"

"My, my, are we bossy today," said Mildred shaking her head.

After much debate, the girls agreed that a nice headband was the way to go for Amanda. They both looked very nice and felt pretty good about themselves. They boosted each other's self-esteem by telling each other how pretty they looked.

"You look like a princess, Amanda," said Mildred.

"Awww. You look like a princess too, Milly."

"Yeah right. I don't know of any princess as big as me," said Mildred a bit disappointed, but seeking reassurance.

"You do too look like a princess, Milly."

"Oh yeah, and what princess is that?"

"You look like Princess Fiona."

"Who's Princess Fiona?"

"Forget it," said Amanda giggling, "Let's go check out what everybody else is doing."

The girls went downstairs. Eric came home and immediately went for the shower. He warned the girls that if they wanted to go with him to pick up Bo, then they needed to be ready in a half an hour. This was not a problem for them. They were elated and ready to go.

When Eric was done, they all went out to get Bo. They went in the family car. This way, they could drive Bo back to the house he'd be staying in.

Meanwhile, at Bo's camp, Bo was all ready to go. He had spent all morning gathering the little belongings he had, including his tent, and saying goodbye to his homeless neighbors. Although he felt bad for them, he knew that it was his time to move on. An opportunity like this would not come around again in a million years. Bo's heart swelled up with gratitude and hope as he saw Eric come for him.

The house Bo was to stay in was about ten miles away from the Muses'. They drove to the house and when they got there, Eric instructed Bo on all of his responsibilities as an employee. Bo was to clean up, check for loose screws and knickknacks, cover up holes on the walls, and paint. Bo would also be responsible for maintaining the lawn and doing some yard work. In return, he would be able to use the house to sleep and shower. He was to get a salary like the rest of the employees.

The only thing that Eric did not want Bo to do there was to cook or use the stove. This was to prevent a fire. Eric told him that he would supply Bo with basic food items that did not require cooking, such as cereal, milk, canned goods, bread, and cold cuts. He was to begin work after the Thanksgiving break.

Obviously, Bo did not have a problem with this and was very happy to accept. After all, this was the best home he'd been in, in a long time. He was also well aware that this was temporary and that it was the first step to finally leaving the vagabond lifestyle. Bo always kept in mind that he promised Eric and himself not to let anybody down.

After directing Bo to the bathroom, Eric gave Bo his new wardrobe and some toiletries such as soap, shampoo, shaving accessories, deodorant, toothpaste, a toothbrush, and an Old Spice cologne that Eric never used. Eric also recommended that Bo get rid of his old clothes. He reminded Bo that in order to receive new things, he needed to get rid of the old ones. Bo was more than happy to get rid of his old clothes. He wanted nothing to do with anything that reminded him of his life in the park. Some of his sweaters still had Coco's hair on them, which made it even harder for him to move on.

"After you're done, Victoria can give you a haircut if you want to," said Eric.

"Yeth, zir. Again, thank you zo much, zir."

"Call me Eric, my friend."

"Eric, I'll be done in no time."

Bo went to take his bath. Eric and the girls eagerly waited for Bo to come out of the shower. They couldn't wait to see him all cleaned up and smelling good. Mildred was impressed by all of Eric's generosity.

"You're an angel, Mr. E," she said.

Chuckling, he replied, "I hardly think so, Mildred."

"But you're so nice!"

"Girls, I do my best to be the best version of me that I can, but don't think for one second that I'm a saint because I'm not. I'm human and I do make mistakes. The important thing to remember is to always have that hunger to improve and grow, and you can only do this by being responsible, honest, giving 110 percent in everything you do, and most of all, being humble. You girls got me?"

"Yes sir," the girls said simultaneously.

About forty minutes later, Bo opened the bathroom door and when he did, all the steam came out as if he had been in a sauna. It had been so long that Bo had taken a warm shower that he milked every drop of hot water. When he lived in the park, he was able to use a public shower in a homeless shelter for $3.00. Whenever he could, he showered there, only the hot water was always limited. There were always other homeless people using it and the hot water would run out fast.

Once the fog cleared, Bo came out looking tall and handsome. He looked like another man. He had put on his 'dressy' pants and shirt for the special occasion. He had shaved and combed his hair back. He had such a big knot in his throat that he couldn't even speak. He wanted to say 'thank you' just one more time, but he couldn't do it without choking up.

When Eric noticed Bo's eyes tearing up, he placed his hand on Bo's shoulder and said, "It's okay, man. No worries."

Bo swallowed and breathed. When he was able to speak, he said, "Let'th go. We don't want to keep Victoria waiting."

The whole day was going as planned. The house smelled of turkey, apples, and cinnamon. The gang arrived home and Vicky could not believe her eyes.

"Oh my god, Bo! Is that you?"

"It ith I, my friend."

"Sweet Jesus, look how great you look!"

"Yeth, Vicky, I cannot thank your family enough."

"Don't be silly, Bo, have a seat and make yourself at home. Dinner will be ready in no time."

"Mmmm, it sure thmellth great!" said Bo.

Amanda and Mildred sat with Bo to keep him company. They invited Junior to sit with them. The first thing Junior did was show Bo his hula-hoop and began to spin it around. Incredibly, he was sharing it with Bo and they took turns. Amanda, Mildred, Junior, and Bo all took turns spinning the hula-hoop.

Dinner was ready shortly after. The Muses never had Thanksgiving dinner too late. They always had it early so that they could relax and watch movies the rest of the evening. It was also their tradition to take out their Christmas tree and Christmas decorations right after dinner so that they could put them up the following day. It gave them something to do on Black Friday.

Dinner was set. The table looked simple and beautiful. As tradition would have it, they all bowed their heads to give thanks. Eric always led the family in prayer. Then they each took turns saying something that they were grateful for.

In a nutshell, Eric was thankful for his family. He even included little Kevin who was to join the family in a couple of weeks. This revelation surprised Mildred because she had no idea that Eric had another son outside his marriage. Bo already knew about the whole illegitimate son thing and didn't see the big deal, but to Mildred, this was a surprise, to say the least.

Vicky was thankful for everyone at the table and for being able to help out two perfect strangers. Amanda was grateful for her parents, brother, and Mildred. Mildred was grateful for everything that had happened to her after leaving the hospital. Junior was thankful for his family and his hula-hoop. In Bo's case, there was so much to be grateful for that he was unable to zero in on just one thing. In the end, he was just grateful that he had been given a second chance to a more dignified life.

As soon as they were done saying grace, Mildred could not hold her tongue any longer.

She blurted out, "Who's Kevin?"

Eric, Vicky, and Amanda all looked at each other wondering who will volunteer to answer her question. Eric, realizing that it was his 'bed,' chose to answer it.

"He's my other son, Mildred. He will be joining our family before Christmas."

"Oh, okay."

Even though Mildred was surprised, she did not judge. She figured that the good that Eric had done outweighed the bad.

Contrary to what everybody was thinking, Vicky did not mind the conversation of Kevin whatsoever. However, she felt that this wasn't the time to get into it.

Eager to change the subject, she turned to Bo and said, "So, Bo, do you mind if I ask you a personal question?"

"Let me gueth. You want to know how I ended up being homeleth, right?" said Bo.

"Uhm," Vicky cleared her throat, "Yes, how did you?"

"Everybody wonderth the thame thing. Thadly, motht people athume that one becometh a homeleth perthon becauthe they are low liveth who either do drugth or are too lazy to work. Don't get me wrong, there are many who are that way, but a lot of uth aren't."

There was a silence at the table. Everyone had been guilty of this assumption at least once in their lives. Bo didn't mind it though. It's easy to judge when you don't understand something. Bo wanted to answer their question and enlighten them.

Bo explained that his father died when Bo was eighteen. Bo was then forced to get a job to be able to provide for himself and his mother.

He ended up working at a meat market as a butcher. Four years later, his mother was diagnosed with cancer and died shortly after. Bo was orphaned at the age of twenty-two.

Bo continued to work at the meat market to support himself; however, when it rains, it pours. Just a year after his mother's demise and while he was at work, Bo slipped on animal blood that was on the floor and injured his back, neck, and shoulder. He was unable to return to work because he couldn't lift anything. His pain was so severe that his doctor had to prescribe him some muscle relaxers and narcotics, which are highly addictive. Unable to ease his pain with anything else, Bo quickly became dependent on his medications.

Unable to work, Bo began to fall behind on his rent. Eventually, he was evicted from his home. To make matters worse, his doctor, who suspected that Bo was becoming addicted to the drugs, stopped prescribing them to him. Bo had severe withdrawal symptoms which made it very difficult for anybody to hire him at that time. He began staying at homeless shelters until the little money he had ran out.

By the time Bo was feeling better and had overcome his addictions, he was homeless, hungry, dirty, and smelly. When he went out looking for jobs, he was immediately rejected. Before he knew it, his main focus was to get a decent meal. Everything else became secondary. The next thing he knew, months turned into years; and the longer he was homeless, the harder it became for him to get back on his feet. It wasn't because he was unwilling to work, but because people were unwilling to hire him.

It took this long, twenty-three years to be exact, to catch a break. It was all thanks to this family that was willing to help. He vowed not to take this opportunity for granted and make it work. After losing Coco, Bo felt like he had no reason to live. He soon realized that life went on with or without him. He understood that it was up to him whether or not he went along for the ride.

This was very enlightening for the Muses. They all agreed that having Bo and Mildred made their Thanksgiving extra special. When dinner was over, Eric drove Bo back to his new but temporary place.

They all wanted him to stay for a while, but Bo was eager to leave. A lot had happened to him and there was plenty more to come. He just wanted to make sense of it all, take it all in, and prepare for the promising future ahead.

The rest of the family got comfortable and waited for Eric to return home. When he did, they put on the movie *Airplane!* This movie came out in 1980 and it was the silliest thing they'd ever seen. Afterward, they put on *Airplane II: The Sequel*. After watching it, the girls began to act out different parts of the movie and could not stop laughing.

Shortly after, they all went to bed. On Black Friday, the family always focused on putting up their Christmas tree and all of the Christmas decorations. The family had only one thing to prepare and look forward to, and that was little Kevin's arrival.

CHAPTER 15

· ·

Little Kevin

*A*fter Thanksgiving, life resumed as usual. Bo had gotten the hang of work and made quite an impression on his boss. He was making close to $15 an hour, which was more than most people earned in that area. Aside from doing all of the handyman's work, he was also doing some decorating as well. By the time Bo was done working on the house, it looked amazing. He put so much love and detail into everything he did that it was hard for aspiring buyers to refuse.

When the house was ready to be put on the market, Bo began to look for his own place. Ironically, the only residential area that he could afford was in the Lakewood Terrace Apartments where Mildred and her father lived. They were not very strict about credit or documentation. This made it easy for Bo to get a decent apartment there.

Mildred had her stitches removed and her wound was healing nicely. She also had the chance to call her father. It was a rather long call. They needed to catch up for all the time they had not seen each other. Joe told her that he was doing great and that he couldn't wait to get back home and start over. He had learned to be more open with his feelings and it became easier for him to tell Mildred that he missed her and loved her very much.

At one point in the conversation, Mildred asked Joe about her mom. Joe told her that her mother was doing jail time for possession of illegal drugs, and for withholding and tampering with evidence. She might not have to serve the entire sentence for good behavior, but Joe did not know all of the details. Mildred asked if she could go see her mother. Joe promised that he would take her after he was done with the program.

Mildred told Joe how much fun she was having with the Muses and especially with her best friend, Mandy. She told him all the things that she had learned. Joe could tell how much Mildred had grown and matured just by listening to her speak. He was very happy for her and it gave him even more of a reason to complete the program and never go back to his old drunken ways.

Eric had gotten all of his paperwork ready and officially became Kevin's custodial parent. Vicky and Eric had complete custody of their youngest son. They were both looking forward to having Kevin with them. They couldn't wait. Eric was to go to New York City and pick up little Kevin.

Kevin's biological mother, Susan, did not spend a lot of time with Kevin. Usually, she left Kevin with the nanny. Susan avoided having any real connection with her son because she knew that she would eventually have to give him up. She was not ready to be a single mother nor tell her family in China about her illegitimate son.

Eric flew to New York City on Friday, December 17, 2013. He was so excited that he could almost see his heart trying to escape his chest with every beat. Even though he had a son and a daughter, he had always wanted another child. Vicky had had two very difficult pregnancies and was scared of a third. She was also at an age where it was risky for her to have another baby. This was the perfect scenario for both Eric and Vicky. They got the joy of another child without the difficulty of a pregnancy.

When Eric arrived in New York City, things could not have gone any better. Eric did not have to see Susan at all. She wanted to skip the awkwardness of giving up her own son and the difficult goodbye. Eric dealt directly with the nanny and a social worker who waited for him at the social worker's office.

When father and son saw each other for the very first time, it was magical. They had an instant connection. If there is ever such a thing as love at first sight, this was it. All it took was Eric saying, "Hi Kevin, I'm your daddy."

The minute Kevin heard those words, his whole world made sense. He was so eager to have an actual parent, a father especially, that his natural response was to go for a hug and scream out, "Daddy!" It was so cute that the nanny, the social worker, and anyone who happened to be walking by, broke out crying. There were just not enough tissues to go around. Eric's heart was so full of love in that moment that he thought it was going to burst.

Kevin was such a beautiful little boy. He had beautiful olive skin and Asian features. He was only two, but incredibly, it made perfect sense to Kevin why he looked the way he did when he saw his dad.

The exchange was quick, nice, and easy. The father and son pair were to take the first flight to Denver the next day. Meanwhile, Eric and Kevin took the extra hours of that day to get to know each other better; and what better way to do that than to hang out in New York City around the holidays? Is there a better place in the world to be in around Christmas?

They went to Central Park, Rockefeller Center, St. Patrick's Cathedral, Time Square, the South Street Seaport, and finally to Chinatown. It was all so remarkable; the decorations along Fifth Avenue, the smell of chestnuts roasting in the streets, the big lights, and that New York City pizza which made it all so special. It was sheer magic and awesomeness. Kevin's favorite part was riding on the subway and having New York City pizza. Eric loved hanging out with his beautiful baby boy. He was so proud.

By the time father and son got to the hotel, they were exhausted. The minute their heads hit their pillows, they knocked out. They woke up bright and early the next day and headed out for Denver. Vicky and the rest of the family all went to pick them up at the airport. They had spent the entire day organizing and preparing the house for Kevin; making it childproof and suitable for a two-year-old. They were all so thrilled.

There was an extra bedroom in the house which Eric had converted into his home office. He never used it, so they turned it into little Kevin's room. However, the family agreed to let Kevin sleep in Junior's room or in a toddler bed with the girls until he got used to his new home.

Eric had packed very light and Kevin did not have much either. They were able to travel with carry-on luggage. This meant that when they arrive at Denver airport, they could skip waiting for their luggage. They could just come out of the plane and head straight to their car.

Eric and Kevin were one of the first people to come out of the gate. Eric's eyes watered as he saw his family waiting for him just outside of security. He felt like the luckiest and richest man alive. When the family took one look at Kevin, they melted. Vicky went toward them first. Amanda, Junior, and Mildred instinctively knew that they needed to give the adults and baby some alone time to allow the moment to marinate a little bit.

Vicky went toward her husband and hugged him. Then, she stooped down toward Kevin and said, "Hey, buddy, I've been waiting for you."

Little Kevin looked at her. "Are you my new mommy?"

Those words immediately took Vicky's breath away. With a heart inflated like a balloon and watery eyes, Vicky responded, "Yes. Yes, baby. I am. I am your new mommy."

Kevin let go of his dad's hands and quickly went and hugged Vicky. That was the cue for the rest of the children to run over and meet him.

Eric also stooped down to Kevin's level. "And this here is your brother, Junior, and your sister, Amanda. This is Amanda's friend, Mildred, who's staying with us for a little while."

Everyone was waiting for their turn to hug Kevin. He was just so adorable. Some other airport goers were starting to come out of the exit and the Muses were in their way. Eric gathered his family and instructed everyone to hold their urges to hug and carry Kevin until they get home or at least till they were in the van. Then they would be able to hug and kiss him as much as they'd like.

Once in the van, the goal was to help Kevin remember everyone's name. Because he was only two, Kevin had a cute way of pronouncing their names. He called Amanda "Manda," Junior "Juno," and Mildred "Mid-day."

Mildred was especially enamored with Kevin. Amanda grew up helping Vicky care for Junior and was not very into the whole baby thing. Mildred, on the other hand, had a very maternal heart. She didn't remember, but she always played with dolls and had always craved that maternal figure. She loved little kids. How she dealt with kids was probably a reflection of how she would have wanted to be treated as a child. Even though she didn't remember her past, it was something that she was aware of in her core.

Mildred took a real liking to Kevin, and Kevin to Mildred. She spent the whole ride trying to have small conversations with him even after everyone else got tired of trying.

On the way, they happened to pass by a cemetery. Kevin had seen one before because his nanny frequently went to take flowers to her mother's grave. Many times, she took Kevin with her.

As soon as Kevin saw the graveyard, he said, "Dat's a cementewy!"

Surprised, but amused that a kid his age knew what a cemetery was, Amanda said, "Oh my god, Kevin! Do you even know what a cemetery is?"

"Yes," he said, "It's where the dead people live!"

They were all laughing and aww-ing at the same time. Mildred just wanted to take a big bite out of him.

They finally arrived at their home and the girls showed Kevin around. Meanwhile, Vicky was trying to figure out what to make for lunch. After much thought, she came to the conclusion that her head was not in cooking mode that day. Eric, being the observant husband that he was, suggested that they all go out for pizza. This way, Kevin could have some New York City pizza in Colorado and the family could spend more time with him. With that excellent plan in mind, they went out again.

After pizza, they stopped by the public library to pick up some children's books for Kevin. Everyone went to their own area to look for stuff. Mildred and Amanda went to the computer area and sat in different booths to surf the internet. Out of nowhere, Mildred got her first real flashback. She remembered, for a brief moment, Amanda and the Muse family in the library.

She quickly turned to Amanda and said, "Mandy, Mandy, I remember something! Something's familiar!"

Amanda's heart stopped for a second or two. "What? What's familiar?"

"This! The library, you and your family. Something's very familiar!"

"Maybe it's déjà vu. I can assure you that we have never been in this library all of us together."

"Déjà vu? What the heck is that, Amanda? No, I'm sure I've been here with your family."

"Déjà vu is when you think you've seen something twice. It happens to me all the time. Don't worry about it. You're probably in the matrix or something."

"Matrix?"

"Shhhh!" Amanda whispered, "Just forget it, okay? You're in a library and you're being awfully loud!"

Mildred chose to let it go, but she knew deep down that this was no déjà vu moment. She specifically remembered being in that library and seeing the Muses.

She didn't understand why Amanda would lie about being in the library with her family. It just didn't make any sense. Mildred had so many questions, but she left it alone. She figured that it would all make sense to her someday.

Amanda, on the other hand, was a bit worried. Could it be true? Could Mildred be getting her memory back sooner than she had anticipated? How would Mildred react if she were to find out that she's been tricked? Amanda had not thought of this before. She had grown to love Mildred, not only because she was good company, but because Mildred had become a very nice person with an awesome heart.

After the library, they all went home. They did what they normally do on Saturdays, only this time, they had Kevin. Kevin made everything even more refreshing. Kevin enjoyed his time spinning things with Junior, dancing to 'Hey Mickey' with Vicky, and reading with the girls in their room.

At bedtime, Kevin felt more comfortable in the girls' room. Amanda and Mildred put his little toddler bed next to their beds, but it was pointless. The girls wanted to sleep with him. They had decided on taking turns, no problem. The real problem was deciding who got to sleep with him first. Their decision came down to a rock, paper, and scissors draw in which Amanda came out the victorious winner.

Every night, the girls took turns with Kevin. The bond between Mildred and the Muses grew stronger every day. Mildred often wondered what life would be like once her father came out of rehab and she moved back home with him. Amanda reminded Mildred that she was always welcomed in her home and that they would continue to be best friends forever.

Soon after Kevin's arrival, it was Christmas. The Muses invited Bo over again. It went pretty much the same as Thanksgiving except for the gift exchange. It wasn't a big deal; the usual boxers and tie for Dad, the Bed Bath & Beyond for Mom, cars and trucks for Kevin, MP3 players for the girls, clothes for Junior, and a nice sweater for Bo.

Bo had officially moved into the Lakewood Terrace Apartments where Mildred lived and was doing very well. He had kept his promise of not letting Eric down.

In just a matter of weeks, Bo was given a small promotion. Bo became the official handyman for all the properties. The only thing that he was missing was his dear friend Coco.

Joe was scheduled to be discharged from the rehab program mid-January. Mildred wanted to prepare for that day. She went over to her apartment and had her neighbor, Alice, open the door. She couldn't understand why her apartment looked so dark and gloomy, especially when she compared it to the Muses' home.

Amanda went with her and got a little taste of Mildred's world. Amanda was able to understand a little bit why Mildred was always so miserable. Her apartment was dark in all the rooms. In efforts to save money, Joe only put bulbs in specific areas of the apartment and never saw the need for curtains or anything that would make the apartment more like a home.

The girls decided to go over to Bo for suggestions. He gladly came over and helped them brighten up the place. Bo began by replacing the brown venetian blinds with white ones. Then he put up some nice curtains that Alice had donated to the Riley's, and moved some furniture around. Bo also screwed in some bulbs that were missing all around the apartment. The new blinds, the lighting, and the curtains gave the apartment a whole new and fresh look. They immediately felt a new and positive energy flowing all through Mildred's home.

Mildred thanked Bo for his help and told him that she looked forward to being his neighbor. Bo wondered if she'd feel the same way after she got her memory back. Nevertheless, he let her know that he would be there for her whenever she needed him.

CHAPTER 16

···

Joe's Return

*N*inety days had passed and everyone agreed that it went by pretty fast. It was time for Joe to go back home, reclaim his life, and put everything he learned from the program into practice. This also meant that it was time for Mildred to leave the Muses' home and start her new life with her father. Everyone was sad to see her go, especially Amanda and little Kevin. They had become very close since they shared a room and always had their late night talks. Kevin had become very attached to his big sister 'Mid-day' and she had become very much attached to him too.

The family made sure that Mildred knew that she would be missed. They also thanked her for all she had done for Junior and for babysitting Kevin at times. Vicky told Mildred that she was always welcome in her home. Amanda reminded Mildred that even though bedtime will never be the same without her, they would at least see each other at school. Maybe on the weekends, Mildred could sleep over.

Mildred was also sad to go. She let the Muses know that she would be missing them too. She couldn't thank them enough for their hospitality and everything they had done for her. She admitted that she was a bit scared to move in with her father; after all, Joe was still practically a stranger to her. Mildred had no idea what life would be like with him.

Joe showed up at the Muses' home early Thursday morning. It was so refreshing to see him again. When he came for Mildred, everyone could see the change in him.

Before rehab, Joe was thin, sloppy, and unshaved. He rarely cut his hair and always wore a baseball cap. Even when he showered, he always smelled like motor oil and beer. He was also in a desperate need of a dental cleaning. Aside from having yellow, coffee-stained teeth, he also had a lot of plaque on them. This caused him to have a serious case of chronic halitosis, or as it is commonly known, bad breath. It was obvious that Joe had let himself go. In his high school pictures, one could tell that he was a very good looking guy. It seemed that his troubles really got the best of him.

By the time Joe got to the Muses', everyone noticed how he was clean and shaven. He had gained a little weight and was dressed very nicely with no cap. He no longer smelled funky and he had obviously had some dental work done. Not only did he look like your typical dad, but he was also quite a catch.

Mildred was indisputably very sad to leave, but she was also very happy to see her father change for the better. He looked so different from how she last saw him.

Mildred was very proud of him. Vicky was also very happy and impressed to see the new Mr. Riley. The sense of pride and joy overwhelmed her spirit. She was so happy to know that she somehow contributed to his transformation. Words could not describe the sense of fulfillment Vicky felt.

Mildred and her dad thanked the Muse family one last time and they went home. Mildred had her own little surprise for Joe and couldn't wait to see how he would react to his new place.

When Joe walked into his apartment, he noticed the change right away and he loved it. Their little apartment looked very nice and cozy. Joe was very happy and grateful because he really did not want to come home to the same gloomy place.

He had become a different man, and he didn't think or see things in the same way.

He worried that eventually, the eerie, depressing place would take him back to where he was before rehab. With his home updated and brightened, he almost felt as if they had moved into a new place.

That very day, Joe met Bo, his new neighbor. They hit it off right away. They shared their addiction stories and their enthusiasm for a new start. They had so much in common that they were able to relate to each other very easily. Before treatment, Joe would have found Bo's mannerisms rather offensive, but Joe had made a choice when he was in rehab to disregard all of the pettiness and love people for who they are. With all of the flaws he had, Joe was in no position to judge anybody.

As soon as Joe embraced Bo's personality, Joe gained a wonderful friend. Bo was a friend that would never judge him. In time, Joe found Bo's mannerisms and speech impediment rather amusing and even refreshing. Joe made fun of Bo while Bo made fun of Joe's ruggedness. It was hilarious to see Bo trying to act masculine. He would walk swaying from side to side, holding his crotch and pretending to spit.

Joe and Bo's friendship made it easier for Mildred to adapt to her new place. Having Bo there was like having a little bit of her unforgettable experience with the Muse family. She had accepted Bo as part of her family and she honestly liked it. She was even proud to say that she had two dads, not caring what assumptions people might make. Not caring what people thought and just being herself was very liberating.

Joe was not the most communicative man on earth so the task of sitting down and getting to know his daughter better was not an easy one. For some reason, Joe had forgotten that his daughter had suffered a head injury and that she had amnesia. Sometimes, this would pose a problem because he would talk to her as if the accident never happened. Luckily, Bo was always around to remind him of that and be a middle man for the father and daughter.

One night, Mildred sat down and asked her father if he would answer a couple of questions. She felt the urge to find out more about her past. When she was living with Amanda and her family, her past didn't matter because everything was so perfect that she didn't care about her past. Now that Mildred was alone with Joe, she had more time to think and wonder about it.

Most of Mildred's questions gravitated around her mother. Joe didn't mind these questions about Jennifer. Quite frankly, he preferred to talk about Jennifer instead of getting into how mean Mildred was to her peers before the accident. He liked his daughter's new demeanor and didn't want to ruin it. Mildred, on the other hand, was not very interested in her persona. Mildred didn't care about who she was in the past because she knew who she was at that moment, and she felt comfortable with it.

Basically, Mildred wanted to know in full detail why her mother was in jail and why she had abandoned her. Joe opened his heart to her like he'd never done with anybody else before. For a long time, Joe had been filled with anger and resentment toward Jennifer. He never had anything good to say about her.

The truth was that Jennifer met Joe when she was only seventeen and she married him almost immediately. She came from a broken home where everything was drama, violence, and alcohol. Running off with Joe, who was ten years her senior, was her escape from her miserable life. In the beginning of their relationship, Jennifer stayed with Joe more out of convenience than anything else, but once she had Mildred, she felt that she loved Joe. Unfortunately, that feeling didn't last very long.

Joe had always been a truck driver. His routes had typically been local ones that allowed him to go home every day. Four years after Mildred's birth, money was tight and Joe decided to get a job as a trucker that went further out for his jobs. This meant more money, but less time at home. Jennifer found herself lonely and depressed most of the time, and had to raise Mildred practically on her own. She quickly began to question her life and her marriage with Joe.

One day, she went to the local grocery store and saw Justin, an old friend from her past. Justin went to the same elementary school that Jennifer had, only he was a year younger than her. Justin was very good looking, but like Jennifer, he had not amounted to much. He had dropped out of high school in his freshman year, lived in his grandmother's basement, was unemployed, and began flirting with heroin, meth, and other illegal drugs.

When they saw each other at the store, they felt an instant and mutual attraction.

They exchanged numbers so that they could maybe meet up for coffee one day and catch up on old times. When Jennifer dropped Mildred off at pre-school, she had a lot of free time, especially because her husband was out working. Sometimes, Jennifer was alone for days at a time.

Jennifer secretly began to meet with Justin on a regular basis. By the time she realized that Justin was a big-time loser, it was too late. She had fallen head over heels in lust with him. To make matters worse, she also began to experiment with drugs. Not wanting to drag Mildred into her dark and messy world or ask someone for help, Jennifer left both Mildred and Joe and moved in with Justin.

Two months after moving in with Justin, Jennifer became pregnant. Seven months later, she gave birth to a premature baby boy whom she named Luke. For the most part, Luke was being raised by Lola, Justin's grandmother, because his parents were too busy getting high to care for him.

Not too long into their relationship, they got so involved with drugs that they were unable to support their habit. Unemployment along with a drug problem can lead anyone to do despicable things. It's a very simple equation: unemployment plus addiction equals unthinkable crimes. Inevitably, they began stealing and engaging in petty crimes. Before they knew it, their petty crimes had escalated to more serious and dangerous acts of violence.

One day, the two broke into an old lady's home hoping to find valuable jewelry or money they could use to pay for their next fix. Sadly, the old lady resisted and threatened to call the police. Justin, desperate and scared, picked up a kitchen knife and stabbed the old lady three times, killing her.

Justin was so fixated on getting money for his drugs that he did not care what he needed to do to get it. Jennifer, although shocked by the turn of events, stood by her man. For a split second, she thought of leaving, but she didn't know where to go or what she was going to do without Justin. Unfortunately, Jennifer chose to stay and be a part of this horrific crime. She went as far as taking the knife with her, hoping that police would not find it.

Justin had left so much evidence and so many fingerprints all over the crime scene that the police caught him only two days later. They found him and Jennifer stoned out of their minds in their basement apartment. Justin was charged with second-degree murder, and Jennifer was also arrested for being his accomplice as well as trying to conceal evidence. He was given forty years in prison, and Jennifer was given eight.

Joe told Mildred the whole story except for the fact that she had a six-year-old brother named Luke. The reason that he did not mention Luke was because Joe didn't know about him. The Luke pregnancy happened so fast that it went unnoticed. After Luke was born, he was quickly passed on to his great-grandmother, Lola, and was never seen in public with his own parents.

Joe was so distraught when Jennifer left him that he never bothered to find out about her. He just focused on his work, which served as an escape. He learned of Jennifer's incarceration when Alice saw it on the local news and told him about it.

When Mildred found out about her mother, her first reaction was to feel pain. She did not understand how a mother could be so selfish that they would abandon their own flesh and blood for a man, especially a big loser like Justin. At that point, Mildred felt sorry for her dad and felt grateful for him. Despite his choices, she appreciated that he had stuck around. She hugged him. "I'm so sorry, Dad."

Joe explained to Mildred that he no longer felt resentment toward Jennifer. He admitted that a lot of what happened was his fault. Joe couldn't help to think that if he would have spent more time with his family instead of working all the time, then this would have probably gone in a different direction. Joe confessed that he neglected Jennifer when she needed him the most and he was very sorry for that. Joe promised Mildred that he was not going to do the same to her.

Feeling a little more compassion toward her mother, Mildred asked her father if she could visit her in jail. Joe agreed to take Mildred. Jennifer was to be released in a year or so, but Mildred wanted to see her anyway and Joe did not mind it at all. He too had wanted to face her, and this was the perfect time to do so.

That weekend, as Mildred spent more time in her room, she began to get very small flashbacks here and there. When she played with her dolls, she remembered little episodes where her dolls fought and even killed each other. It all seemed too gruesome, morbid, and scary; she dismissed those thoughts. She couldn't understand all the violence. She assumed that she had been watching too many scary movies at Amanda's house.

The weekend ended and it was time to start a new school week. Before going back to work, Joe wanted to make his new role as a single dad formal by taking Mildred to school and meeting all of her teachers. It was something he had never done before and was frankly, way overdue. All the teachers knew he struggled as a single dad, but that was all they knew about him.

When Joe got to the school, he went to visit Mr. Erickson, Ms. Rogers, Mrs. Dotson, and finally Mrs. Clancy, Mildred's math teacher. When Joe met Mrs.Clancy, Mildred noticed a slight 'glow' to both Joe and Mrs. Clancy. It seemed as if they were being a bit flirtatious with each other. It was not verbal, but it became obvious because they were smiling with their eyes and laughing at each other's corny jokes.

Love does things to people. Mostly, it makes people act idiotic. It doesn't really matter how smart you are; when people are in love, they tend to act foolishly. It's nothing to be ashamed of because it happens to the best of us.

Joe politely excused himself from his meeting with Mrs. Clancy by saying that he knew she needed to get back to teaching. Mrs. Clancy told him that he was no trouble at all and that it was refreshing to see a parent so involved in their child's education. She then walked over to her desk, and on a luminescent pink sticky note, she wrote her full name and phone number and handed it over to Joe.

"Mr. Riley, please feel free to call me if you have any questions or concerns, or if you just need someone to talk to. It must be so difficult for you as a single dad. I know that sometimes you must need a woman's point of view."

All the students, including Mildred, collectively thought the same thing.

"O-kaaay?..."

Amanda was already in class waiting for Mildred. As soon as Mildred sat down next to her, Amanda leaned over toward Mildred and whispered, "Did you see that? What was that all about?"

Mildred giggled. "Relax, Cupid. That was an innocent exchange of personal information."

"Mmhmm. Yeah, okay," said Amanda suspiciously.

Joe said goodbye first to Mildred and Amanda and then to Mrs. Clancy. The entire class was giggling and whispering, and they were all very well aware of the love story that was waiting to happen. They quickly collected themselves and continued with their math class.

At lunchtime, Amanda, Mildred, Lucinda, Daniel, and Sky got together as always. The main topic that day was Mildred, her new home and the possibility that she was going to have Mrs. Clancy as her stepmom. Mildred didn't have much to say. Even though she missed staying at Amanda's house, she looked forward to a bright new future with her dad. She was only interested in two things, and that was to help her father remain sober and to meet her mother. She also loved the idea of having Bo as her neighbor and the option to always be able to go to Amanda's house.

Again, the group could not believe the change they had seen in Mildred. On many occasions, they felt the need to bite their tongues so that they wouldn't tell Mildred how evil she was and how much she had changed. Lucinda, especially, struggled with holding that information in.

As they had their lunch, Lucinda said, "Well, just look at you, Mildred. Who'd ever thought that you'd be sitting here with us, losers?"

Confused, Mildred responded, "What do you mean?"

Before the conversation progressed any further, Amanda said, "You know, after your accident. You know, we thought we almost lost you there, girl. By the way, wanna come over this Saturday? Little Kevin does nothing but ask about you."

"Awww, I miss my little Boo-Boo too. I'll ask my dad, but I'm sure it's fine. He and Bo have become good friends now. Maybe I can give him a break this weekend so that he can go hang out with Bo."

"Cool!" said Amanda.

They spoke a little bit about everything. The only thing that Mildred neglected to mention was that she had been getting small flashbacks of her past. Perhaps she didn't want to say anything because she was unsure if they were legitimate memories or 'déjà vu,' as Amanda had so eloquently stated once before.

Another week went by. Everything was starting to fall into place at the Rileys' home. Joe started working again. This time, he requested to stay local so that he could spend more time at home. He sporadically asked Mildred questions about Mrs. Clancy until it became obvious that he was interested in her.

At the Muses' home, all was well. Little Kevin loved his new family and his new family loved him. It was almost February, and his birthday was coming up on Valentine's Day. He constantly asked for his other big sister 'Mid-day.'

For two consecutive weekends, Mildred had slept over Amanda's house. On Fridays, Mildred would go out for pizza with Joe and then they'd watch a movie. After dinner on Saturdays, she'd go to Amanda's house, sleep over, go to church with the family the following day, and then go home. This became a routine for the families. They felt very comfortable with it. It seemed that life, as they knew it, had reached a perfect bliss. Everybody knew what they had to do and they did it happily. Life was good.

CHAPTER 17

∙∙

The Moment of Truth

*I*t was Monday morning, and it all seemed like any other Monday except that it was very cold out. Winter weather had finally set in. Mildred usually had a bowl of cereal with milk for breakfast, but because the weather was so harsh, she decided to have a hot chocolate and a croissant instead.

On her way to school, she began having a mild but annoying tummy ache. She blamed the hot chocolate. When she got to school, Mildred briefly mentioned to her friends that ever since she had hot chocolate for breakfast, she had been having a tummy ache. During math class, Mildred excused herself to go to the restroom. She began having cramps and felt as if she may have diarrhea or something.

When Mildred sat on the toilet, she pulled down her pants and underwear only to get the surprise of her life. Does anything sound familiar? Mildred had officially reached puberty and had gotten her period on this cold winter's day.

Mildred had no idea what a menstrual cycle was even before she had lost her memory. Joe had never spoken to her about it, and the little heart-to-heart talk he had with her did not include 'the talk' either. The first time she was ever exposed to this knowledge was when Amanda publicly got her period in the cafeteria. That whole bloody scene was very traumatic for Mildred.

At first, Mildred did not know what to think. It just didn't make any sense.

Why would she bleed out of nowhere? Then, all of a sudden, her mind felt cool, like when you take a warm hat off. It was almost the same feeling you get when your ears are clogged up for a long time and it pops all of a sudden. The blood in front of her smacked her right on the face, and in a snap of the fingers, Mildred regained her memory—*all of it.*

This was neither a flashback nor déjà vu. Mildred Riley had regained all of her memory. The sight of blood on her underwear affected her in the same way it did when Amanda got her period for the first time. *"I got my period just like Bloody Mandy. Oh my god!"* she thought.

Mildred had to put her hand over her jaw to prevent it from dropping.

"Amanda is Bloody Mandy! Oh my god! Amanda isn't my friend!" As reality started to slowly set in, she realized, not only who she was, but who Amanda was as well.

"Amanda is the girl that I hated so much and now- Oh my god!"

Mildred was in a total state of shock. She was confused and had no idea of what to do. This person who had been posing as her 'BFF' was actually the girl that Mildred had been picking on since the beginning of the school year. She felt terrible! She almost wanted to go back to where she didn't remember a thing.

"Amanda must hate me so much! Why would she pose as my best friend?"

This was all that was racing through Mildred's head at that moment and none of it made any sense.

"Amanda has been telling me that she is my best friend to get back at me somehow! And Lucinda, Gassy Lucy, I have been picking on her for years! She is also in on this lie. She hates me too and wants revenge! No wonder she keeps saying little things like, 'Look at you sitting with us.' My friends—they are not my friends! Liz is my only friend, but why is she...?"

Mildred was as confused as a cheap watch.

"Is it possible that after mistreating people for so long they would forgive me so easily? No, I don't think so. I'm sure she hates me, everybody does! Somehow they are all plotting some kind of revenge against me!"

Mildred clearly remembered her hate toward Amanda, only now she understood that all this time she had been hating her for no reason at all. Mildred began to understand that she was envious of Amanda and that was why she bullied her so much. She was able to remember her miserable life at home with the old Joe and how lonely and miserable she felt. Mildred could not understand why Amanda chose to lie about them being so close.

Bit by bit, all the pieces of the puzzle started to come together.

"If I was so mean to her, why did she go see me at the hospital? Wait a minute—why was I in the hospital?" she continued her wrecking train of thoughts.

"Oh my god, Bo! Bo hit me with that ro—"

Mildred couldn't even finish her thought. It was so devastating. Her entire world was crashing down right before her, so much so that she had forgotten about her period. Everything she knew after coming out of the hospital, her perfect and happy life, was nothing but a big, fat lie. Nothing was real.

Mildred remembered being expelled from school the day of the accident, but she couldn't figure out why she was allowed back. Could it be that the teachers were also in on this horrific joke? It was like she was living in the twilight zone.

She felt so stupid, so cheated, so betrayed. She had no idea what she was going to do next.

Well, there was nothing to do but to clean up and run to the counselor's office.

She placed a lot of rolled up toilet paper on her underwear to make sure that the blood did not seep through her clothes, and then she went to see Mrs. Dotson.

When she got to the school's main office, she barged into Mrs. Dotson's office which was located inside the main.

Out of breath and hysterical, she said, "Mrs. Dotson, Mrs. Dotson, help me, help me please!"

"Mildred! What is going on? What is the matter?"

It was on the tip of Mildred's tongue to tell Mrs. Dotson that she had regained her memory, but then she chose to wait just a bit longer. She felt that she needed to sort some things out before saying anything. There were just too many questions on her mind.

"I got my period!" she said trying to tone it down a bit.

"My goodness, Mildred Riley, you scared the bejesus out of me! For cryin' out loud, it's only your period! This is normal for a girl your age. Now you sit here and I'll go get you a sanitary pad. Would you like me to call your father?"

"Um, no. I'll tell him when I get home."

"Good enough. Now sit yourself down, young lady, while I go get you that pad."

Mrs. Dotson gave Mildred the pad and directed her to the restroom next to her office. After Mildred put it on, she went back to class. She decided not to say anything regarding her memory until lunchtime. This would give her some more time to think about everything.

When she returned to class, Amanda leaned over and whispered to her, "Are you okay?"

"Yes, I'm okay. I just got my period though," Mildred whispered back.

"No frikin' way!" said Amanda.

"Amanda, Amanda Muse, is there a problem?" asked Mrs. Clancy.

"No, ma'am," said Amanda.

As soon as Mrs. Clancy drew her attention back to teaching, Mildred leaned over toward Amanda and whispered, "I'll tell you all about it at lunchtime."

"Okay," Amanda whispered back.

After that, Mildred had spent all of math class and all of the other classes that followed, thinking about everything that was happening to her. The more she thought about, the angrier she got and the more hurt she felt. She couldn't believe how fake everybody was being toward her. What hurt her the most was that she genuinely loved her friends, Amanda's family, and her new life in general. But nothing was real; everything was a big, fat lie. Mildred reached a point of contemplating revenge. What if she didn't say anything and just played along, or figure out a way to get even with everybody? This was all too devastating.

At lunchtime, they all got their lunches and went to sit where they usually sat. Everyone, especially Amanda, noticed that Mildred had been a bit quiet and pensive during class. However, Amanda assumed that it was because of her period. Amanda knew all too well about PMS and moodiness during a menstrual cycle.

Amanda kicked off the conversation by saying, "So Milly, how was your—"

"Oh shut it, Amanda!" Mildred interrupted. She couldn't hold it in any longer.

"Huh?" said Amanda surprised.

The rest of the gang was also wondering what was going on.

"The jig is up! You can stop pretending now," said Mildred.

At this point, Mildred was turning red and Amanda knew she was serious. Amanda just didn't understand why Mildred was reacting the way she was. Amanda got so used to the new Mildred that she had forgotten that the old Mildred existed altogether.

Lucinda, on the other hand, began to suspect that maybe Mildred had recovered. She went to Amanda's defense and said, "Mildred, what are you talking about? Why are you so upset?"

"You too, Gassy Lucy! All of you! You can all stop pretending now!" Mildred yelled at the top of her lungs.

Before you knew it, the entire cafeteria had their eyes on what was going on. The whole student body collectively stopped chewing their food and just stared at the scene in utter silence, frozen. They were waiting to see what was going to happen next. Even Liz, who was sitting with her new best friend, Sharon, was feeling the tension. You could almost hear a pin drop.

In the dead silence, Liz turned to Sharon very slowly and very softly said, "I knew this was going to happen sooner or later."

Mildred looked around at the entire school and realized that everyone knew and that everyone was in on what she considered to be a really cruel joke. From kids she barely knew, to teachers, staff, and close friends. Mildred's face became visibly ravaged by grief.

At this point, Amanda had nothing. The jig was up. Amanda also felt devastation. It killed her to see that pain in a person whom she had grown to love. She did not see this coming at all. Amanda did not anticipate the consequences of her plan in the least. It was going so well that she assumed that it would all be perfect in the end. Heck, she had even forgotten how this whole mess started.

Even though Mildred was hurt with everyone, the person she could not stop looking at was Amanda. She felt most hurt and indignation toward her. Mildred looked at Amanda one last time. With a defeated spirit and a breaking voice, she said, "Why, Mandy? Why?"

Amanda could tell that Mildred wanted to cry. Her eyes watered up. The worst part was that Amanda had nothing to say. Nothing she could have said would have eased Mildred's pain. She opened her mouth and hoped that something soothing would come out of it, but it didn't.

"Milly I—"

"I was your friend, Amanda, and I believed you were mine. I learned to love you and your family, and all this time you were lying to me. I know I haven't been good to you in the past, but you went too far, Amanda. You went too—"

Mildred couldn't finish her sentence. She choked up and began to cry. Mildred was too embarrassed to stick around. She put her hands on her face and ran out the cafeteria like a bat out of hell. As she ran and made it to the school hallway, she stopped half way because she realized that she did not know where she was going. She felt so alone. The only place that would make sense for her to go was to Mrs. Dotson's office, and so she did. Luckily, Mrs. Dotson always had her lunch in her office.

When Mildred got to Mrs. Dotson's office, Mrs. Dotson was having her bacon, lettuce, and tomato sandwich. She also had a chicken soup, an Arizona iced tea, and a banana that she would have for dessert.

When Mrs. Dotson saw Mildred walking in, she told her right away, "Mildred, I'm on my lunch break and unless this is an emergency, you need to—"

"I really need to speak to somebody, Mrs. Dotson!" Mildred said hysterically. Mrs. Dotson noticed that Mildred had been crying and agreed to let her in. She immediately got up and locked her door.

"What is it, dear? What is going on?" said Mrs. Dotson not sure of what Mildred was going to say.

"Tell me something, Mrs. Dotson, did you know? Did you know that everyone was pretending to like me to somehow get back at me for being so mean to them?"

"Oh, honey, whatever do you mean?" said Mrs. Dotson with her hand on her chest overdramatizing. Mrs. Dotson was a terrible actress.

"I got my memory back, Mrs. Dotson. You can stop pretending now. I was in the bathroom earlier and I started remembering everything. I remember being really mean to everybody and now I don't understand why everyone is being so nice to me all of a sudden. Is this part of a really sick joke? Did you know about this?"

Mrs. Dotson took a deep breath. As she exhaled she said, "Oh, my dear child, yes. I did. I knew."

"Why? Why did the entire school, even the teachers, gang up on me?"

"Nobody ganged up on you, Mildred. To be honest, the day you had the accident, you were already expelled from school, and most people here were happy and relieved to see you go. Amanda, who was the person you bullied the most, thought that if we made you believe that you were somebody else, you would stop being a bully and even have a chance at a better life. And it worked! She was right! Just look at you, Mildred, you now have friends, everybody likes you, and you're doing great in school. Your life has never been better! Do you remember how miserable you were before the accident? Can you remember that?"

"Look, Mrs. Dotson, I know that I was not the nicest person in the world, and I'm also willing to admit that my life is so much better now and stuff, but why lie? Why lie for so long? After I had gotten close to everyone, why didn't they just tell me the truth? I mean, how long was everybody going to wait before telling me? And why is Amanda so nice to me when I was so cruel to her? For all I know, she probably did this to protect her friend Bo from getting in trouble. Think about it! She had to be protecting Bo, and that's why she made the whole thing up, so Bo wouldn't go to jail for almost killing me!"

"Mildred, I don't know who Bo is or why Amanda came up with this plan. I don't even know what made everyone agree to it! The only thing I know is all the good that came out of it. Listen, sweetheart, you've been through a lot today. I am going to call your father and let you go home. There's a lot to tell him today and you're going to need the time. Go get your belongings while I call your dad to come get you, okay?"

"Thank you, Mrs. Dotson. I do feel like I want to go home. I'm not sure if my dad can pick me up, but I'd like to go home anyway."

"Okay," said Mrs. Dotson, "Go get your things and I'll notify your dad anyway."

Mildred went to get her belongings to go home. When she arrived back to Mrs. Dotson's office, Mrs. Dotson had already spoken to Joe. She didn't go into details.

Basically, she told Joe that Mildred was not feeling very well and that she wanted to go home. Joe explained that he was finishing up with his last route and that he would be getting home soon. He told Mrs. Dotson that Mildred had his permission to walk home by herself if she wanted to.

Meanwhile, in the cafeteria, everyone gathered in one area to talk about what had happened. That day, the entire school had lunch together. Even after they were all done eating, they continued to talk about it outside in the schoolyard. Everyone felt united by a common cause. Everyone kept zeroing in on Amanda since she was the mastermind behind this operation. Everybody wanted to know what she planned to do next.

But Amanda was scared, afraid to lose her friend. "I don't know! Just leave me alone, please! I'll think of something," she said in frustration.

The truth was that, as much as Amanda said that she would 'think of something,' Amanda could not think of anything. The ability to think of what to do next was interrupted by the feeling of hurt and pain she felt for Mildred. She felt afraid that she would lose her for good. She genuinely felt bad for Mildred. Despite all of Mildred's abuse in the past, Amanda understood that Mildred was no longer that bully.

After her memory loss, Mildred was a totally different person. She had become a caring and gentle giant. Mildred was no longer that big, scary girl in school that was full of rage and envy. She didn't blame the world for her miserable life. Quite the opposite, she had become the type of person who saw the best in people and embraced the not so good. Mildred had learned that everyone was fighting their own demons and that people should be loved and accepted for who they are, regardless of their circumstances. She also learned that we are all pretty much the same in that we are all 'under construction' and we have no right to judge or interrupt God's process in anybody's life.

Amanda grew to love and care for Mildred and so did her family. They all respected the individual that Mildred had become. Now, that wonderful person was walking around defeated and with her heart broken into a thousand pieces. Amanda felt so guilty and so wrong. She couldn't wait to get home. Maybe she could get some advice from her mother, or better yet, from Bo. He knew the entire story from beginning to end.

Amanda was so lost. The only thing she knew for sure was that if Mildred did not forgive her, her life was never going to be the same ever again.

CHAPTER 18

∙∙

Redemption

*M*ildred went straight home that day. She was hoping to bump into someone to talk to, but she didn't. Bo was working and so was everybody else. When she got home, she sat in the living room staring at the wall. That time alone gave Mildred the opportunity she needed to gather all of her thoughts. For a brief moment, she considered speaking to Alice, but she feared that Alice wouldn't understand.

Amanda had the remaining half of the school day ahead of her and it felt like it dragged forever. The entire time she was feeling miserable. At times, she got a little distracted with class, but when the thought of Mildred occasionally popped in her head, Amanda could feel her heart tighten up. This happened quite a lot throughout the day. She hated feeling that way. She felt Mildred's pain on so many levels that it was unbearable. She felt so bad for lying to her for so long. Amanda wished she had told Mildred the truth sooner and not let this go on for so long. She needed to come up with some explanation as to why she was not honest with her, but how do you apologize for something like this?

To make matters worse, Valentine's Day and Kevin's birthday was coming up. Eric and Vicky had planned to take the kids, including Mildred, to a family entertainment center that day after school.

Once there, the kids would be able to play and have pizza and cake. Afterward, Eric planned to take his wife out for a romantic Valentine's Day dinner, and Bo would keep an eye on the kids for a couple of hours.

Amanda had been looking forward to this for a long time. It was not going to be the same without Mildred. Amanda was also afraid that Kevin was going to be asking for Mildred and wondering where she was. Amanda knew she needed to do something. She needed to do something and do it quick. She couldn't wait to get out of school and seek advice.

Finally, the school day came to an end. Amanda walked home as fast as she knew how. She didn't want to walk over to Bo's because she knew he'd be at work. She decided to go home and speak to her mother. Vicky would understand and give her good advice. Amanda was so consumed with worry that before she knew it, she had arrived home.

As Amanda walked into her house, she was gasping for air.

When she was able to catch her breath, she yelled, "Ma! Maaa!"

"Sweet Jesus, Amanda! What's wrong, honey?" said Vicky.

"Mom, we need to talk. I need to talk." Amanda was hysterical.

"Honey, calm down! Talk to me, sweet pea, you're scaring me!"

Without warning, as soon as Amanda opened her mouth and intended to say something, a waterfall of tears rushed down her face. Amanda had no idea where it came from. It was like a typhoon or a flash flood. She had yet to shed a single tear until someone was willing to listen to how she was feeling. She had so much to say that she did not even know where or how to begin. She put her hands on her face and began to cry uncontrollably. Naturally, Vicky was very concerned.

She picked up her daughter's face and said firmly, "Amanda Muse, you tell me what is going on this instant!"

Amanda, barely able to speak, managed to say, "She knows, Mom, she knows! She hates me! What am I going to do?"

Vicky knew immediately what Amanda was talking about.

Vicky hugged her and in a very comforting voice, she said, "Oh honey, I'm so sorry."

"I don't know what to do, Mom, she hates me!" Amanda was wailing, trying really hard to sniff and wipe her tears.

"Oh, honey, I'm sure she doesn't hate you. She's just hurt, that's all. Give her some time to think things through."

"I want to apologize, Mom, but I don't know what to say."

"There's nothing to say but that you are sorry. If you try to explain or justify yourself, your apology is not valid."

"What if she never wants to speak to me again?"

"Now you listen to me, Amanda Muse. Mildred cares about you just as much as you care about her. There's no way that she will not speak to you again. All she needs right now is some time, give her that."

"What about Kevin's birthday, Mom? What if she's not done thinking things through by then?"

"I will call Mildred myself and invite her. She will not say no to me."

With that, Amanda calmed down a bit. She was tempted to call Mildred, but she decided to take her mother's advice and give Mildred some time.

Back at the Riley's, Joe came home to also find his daughter crying on the couch. When he asked her what was wrong, Mildred told him everything: from her getting her period to regaining her memory. She explained how hurt she was that everybody, including the adults, had conspired against her. She also let Joe know that Bo was responsible for her injury. Joe couldn't believe it.

Joe suggested that Mildred would go take a warm shower and relax a bit while he went out to buy 'feminine products' for her. Joe reassured Mildred that everything was going to be fine. He even promised Mildred to take her to see her mother that weekend. That gave Mildred something to look forward to.

Eventually, Mildred got tired of thinking about everything that had happened. Thinking about it over and over was not helping; in fact, it only made it worse. She couldn't find any good reason in her mind that would justify what Amanda did to her. Even worse, why did the adults agree to play along?

That night, both Amanda and Mildred went to bed early. Neither one of them felt like doing anything else. What they normally did after school was of no interest to them. They both felt so miserable that they just wanted the day to end. They both figured that perhaps sleeping would numb the pain. Before going to sleep, they both prayed. Amanda prayed for guidance while Mildred prayed for comfort and answers. They prayed until they finally fell asleep.

It was a long night for both girls, but it was finally over. When Mildred woke up the next day, her strength was completely renewed. She decided to give Amanda the benefit of the doubt and allow her to explain herself. After all, what other choice did she have? Amanda, on the other hand, did not even want to return to school. She was too afraid to face Mildred. She did not know what to expect from Mildred. She also felt very embarrassed.

Nevertheless, they both made it to school. Coincidently, they both got to school a little earlier than usual. Both Amanda and Mildred were so caught up in their emotions that they had skipped breakfast altogether. This was great because it gave them those extra minutes that they needed to talk before class.

Mildred got to school first. She was most eager to get there. She waited by Amanda's locker hoping that Amanda would come early or at least before Lucinda did. As luck would have it, she did. Amanda noticed Mildred standing by her locker and her heart sank. There was nowhere to run or hide. Amanda was going to have to face this giant one way or another.

When Amanda approached Mildred, she said in a very sad, low, and shaky voice, "Hi, Mildred."

"Tell me just one thing, Mandy," Mildred said in a stern voice as if she didn't care about anything else that Amanda could possibly say, "Why?"

Amanda dropped her bag and took the deepest breath she had ever taken. As she was about to speak, Mildred interrupted her and said, "I trusted you! I considered you my sister more than a friend! How could you? How could you do this to me? I know I haven't been the nicest person to you, but why didn't you just leave me in that hospital and let me be? Why did you make me believe that I was this awesome person that everyone loved when in fact, it's the complete opposite? Nobody likes me—everyone hates me! Why, Amanda, why?

"Mildred, I am so sorry," said Amanda, "I never intended for this to happen."

"Then what did you intend? What were your intentions, Amanda?"

"I don't know!" Amanda responded in frustration.

"I was scared for many reasons! That day in the park, you came at me and Bo, talking smack as you always did, and then Bo lost it and well, then I was scared for Bo. It wasn't his fault. His dog had died that day and you came at the wrong time. And when I found out that you were not going to remember a thing, I thought that maybe we could be friends."

"But, why? Why would you want to be my friend? All I've ever done is tease you and hate you since the very first day of school. I don't get it, Amanda. Why would you want to be friends with somebody like that?"

"I don't know! I guess I wanted to understand why you hated me so much. I figured that if you got to know me, you wouldn't hate me so much. Since I couldn't come up with a good reason why you were so mean to me, I assumed that maybe people were mean to you. I thought that if maybe people were really nice to you, you would be nice to everybody else."

Mildred sighed and paused for a few seconds. It just dawned on her how miserable she really was before the accident. For the first time, she realized how angry she was at her mother for abandoning her and her father for not being there all the time. This resentment toward her parents made Mildred hate everyone who had, what she considered to be, a 'normal' family. For the first time, Mildred felt remorse for acting the way that she did. As she looked at Amanda, she realized how much she hated this beautiful person only because she seemed to have a perfect life.

Mildred needed to come face to face with her mother once and for all, now more than ever. This anger toward her mother was the root of all of her darkness and negativity. It stole her peace, it took her joy. If she wanted to defeat those demons forever, then she needed to face them head-on and grab the bull by the horns. Amanda had nothing to do with Mildred's relationship with her family. She was just an innocent bystander. Mildred finally reached a breaking point.

"You know what, Amanda?" Mildred said with tears in her eyes, "I am so sorry for being such a jerk to you all this time. You never did anything to me and yet I treated you so badly. You didn't deserve being humiliated the way I humiliated you. Nobody does."

Amanda, filled with relief, said, "I'm sorry too, Mildred, I really am. I'm sorry for not telling you the truth sooner."

"It's okay, Mandy. To be honest, I doubt I would have reacted any differently."

"I'm still sorry," insisted Amanda.

Right when the girls were exchanging their apologies, Lucinda arrived at her locker, which she shared with Amanda.

When she heard Amanda apologizing, she said loudly, "This, still? Come on, Mildred, get over it! So Amanda played you, yes! She played you like a ukulele, but so the hell what? Look at you! You're happy now! You've got friends and all these people who love you! What the hell, Mildred?"

Mildred started laughing at Lucinda's assumptions.

Once Lucinda was done rambling, Mildred turned to her and said, "Relax, Gassy Lucy, it's okay now. I get it!"

Lucinda could tell that Mildred was joking around. She also sensed a lighter air surrounding them.

"Gassy Lucy? Didn't Amanda take that title away from me with her farts? Didn't you say that she had farted so hard and loud that you were afraid that she was going to take off and launch like a rocket or something?"

"Oh stop it!" said Amanda.

"You know, you have a point, Lucinda. That fart is pretty hard to beat, isn't it, Gassy Mandy?" said Mildred looking at Amanda.

"If I get the 'Gassy Mandy' title, I am honoring you with the 'Bloody Milly' one," said Amanda.

"Okay, can you guys hug and make up now?" suggested Lucinda. Amanda and Mildred did just that.

"Oh, one more thing," said Mildred, "Will you come with me to go visit my mom?"

"It depends," said Amanda, "Will you come to Kevin's birthday party on Friday?"

"Heck yeah! I wouldn't miss it for the world. That's my little Boo!"

"Awesome! All right, let's go to class before you bleed out," said Amanda, teasing Mildred about her period.

"You know what, Mandy? We are running a little late for class. Do you think that if Lucinda and I climbed on your back, you can fart-rocket us to class?" said Mildred.

"Ha, ha, ha, very funny Mildred, very funny," said Amanda.

All three girls laughed and teased each other all the way to their class. This time, it was a fun and playful kind of tease. They had learned what their limits were and how to embrace their 'flaws.' They took each other's mishaps and made light of it, all in good humor. That day turned out to be a great day at school. Mildred and Amanda were happy they had made up.

During lunchtime, Mildred confronted Liz. She wanted to know why Liz didn't go see her at the hospital and why Liz was so quick to stop being her friend. Realizing that Mildred was no longer that troublesome bully, Liz was completely honest with her. Liz explained that their friendship was based on fear and convenience more than anything else. Liz did humbly apologize and Mildred understood. Mildred remembered how nasty she was to people. She did not blame Liz at all and wished her the best.

The week went on and everything was great. Mildred had gone over to Bo's and told him that she had regained her memory and that she remembered everything that happened the day he threw the rock at her. Mildred thanked Bo because he had literally knocked some sense into her. She even apologized for being so mean to him.

Kevin's birthday came and everything went as planned. The kids had a great time at the party and Eric and Vicky went to their romantic Valentine's Day dinner. The very next day, Joe took Mildred to see her mother. It was a very big and exciting day for Mildred, and Amanda was right there for moral support.

Jennifer was not expecting to see her daughter ever again or at least while she was incarcerated. After a while, she had lost hope. Needless to say, she was ecstatic to see her daughter and even Joe. Mildred learned that her mother would be released in just eighteen months. Mildred also learned that she had a six-year-old brother named Luke who was living with his paternal great- grandmother. The news made Mildred very happy. She vowed to go meet him as soon as she got back in town.

Jennifer poured her heart out and even apologized to Mildred for leaving her. She also apologized to Joe and admitted that she could've handled their marital problems differently. She blamed it on her immaturity.

While incarcerated, Jennifer got her GED and did everything she could to better herself. She did often wonder if she would be able to get back into society as a contributing citizen. Jennifer knew how difficult it was for ex-convicts to get jobs.

Mildred opened up as well. She told her mother her whole life story and how much she had changed after losing her memory. She explained how happy she was after she made some great friends and after her father got back on track. Jennifer was surprised to see how her daughter had such a great understanding of love, compassion, and forgiveness. Also, how Mildred was able to turn her life around.

Jennifer's time with her family was up. Mildred had made her peace with her mother and so did Joe. They said good-bye and Mildred promised her that she would visit her more often. This gave Jennifer more fuel to continue working hard at being a better person.

It was around three o'clock when they arrived back in town, and Mildred begged and pleaded with Joe to take her to see her little brother, Luke, if only for a few minutes. Joe was hesitant, but agreed anyway. As it turned out, Luke did not live very far from them at all, maybe fifteen minutes away. He lived in the old house where Jennifer once lived.

Luke's great-grandmother was not very old. She was only sixty-four, but you could tell that she was worn out; mainly because after raising her own kids, she was stuck raising Luke's father, Justin, and now she was raising Luke. The woman never stopped raising kids, and she did it all by herself. Lola had been widowed at the age of forty-eight and never remarried.

Mildred, Joe, and Amanda arrived at Lola's house. She didn't know who they were, but Joe quickly introduced himself and the girls. Lola was very pleased to meet them and invited them in. Lola had a toy poodle that had recently given birth to a litter of four puppies. She kept them downstairs in the basement. She called Luke, who was down in the basement playing with the puppies. Luke ran up the stairs, eager to meet the strangers. They rarely had people over so he was always excited to see new faces.

Luke was very cute. He had dark-brown hair and green eyes. Even though his looks came mostly from his dad, he did look a little like Mildred. He had Mildred's nose and round face. Luke was a very hyperactive kid. Luke was filled with energy.

It was more than obvious that he was a handful.

He came up holding one of the puppies. Lola first introduced him to his big sister, Mildred. He wasn't sure what was going on, so he quickly shifted his attention to the puppy.

As he looked around and saw that he had everyone's undivided attention, he said, "This is my doggie. His name is Denver. I have three more downstairs. Wanna see them?"

For a kid his age, Luke was very outspoken. He spoke very clearly and with a clear sense of knowledge of what he was talking about. Mildred and Amanda could not decline his invitation. Everyone ended up going down to the basement to see the puppies. They were all so adorable. The guests soon learned that Lola would not be able to keep all of the puppies. She needed to give three of them away. Mildred and

Amanda immediately thought of Bo. They begged Lola to let them have a puppy for Bo. Lola agreed without hesitating.

Luke was sad to know that he'd be giving up one of his puppies. Mildred promised him that she would take him to visit the puppy whenever he wanted to. While Mildred probably wasn't going to be able to make good on her promise, it was enough to make Luke more flexible with the idea of giving up the puppy.

After playing with Luke and the puppies, it was time for them to go home. Lola told Mildred that she was welcome anytime. In fact, she encouraged her to visit more often. That way, little Luke would have someone else to talk to. Mildred was happy to know that she could assume the big-sister role through Luke and she was very much looking forward to it.

The weekend ended and it was a great one for everybody. Mildred saw her mother and met her brother. Amanda and Mildred made up and Bo got a new puppy. He named her 'Nechi' because he had sneezed and instead of saying 'ah-choo!' he made a noise that sounded like he had said, 'ne-chi!' Immediately after sneezing, the pup ran to him. From there on, every time Bo said 'Nechi,' the pup ran to him as if she knew that Nechi was her name.

At the Riley's, things just kept getting better. Joe and Mildred needed to adapt to many changes. Be that as it may, they were becoming very comfortable with those changes and even welcomed them. Every time they came across difficult times, they became closer to each other, mostly because they were learning how to communicate better.

At the Muse's home, things went as usual. Vicky was getting used to being a new mom while Eric worked hard to provide for his family. Amanda and Junior helped out with Kevin and were happy to have him around. On the weekends, Mildred would come over and join them as well. On special occasions and on holidays, the Muses, the Riley's, and Bo would meet to celebrate together. Sometimes they alternated homes, but for the most part, they all went to the Muse's home because they had the bigger place.

It was an amazing stroke of luck that brought this bunch together. They all felt alone at one point, even the Muses. The Muse family was fairly new in town and only knew each other. Joe drove a truck all by himself and had very little interaction with anybody, and Bo, well, he was in a place where everyone was looking out for themselves. These strangers joined forces and became family. What a beautiful thing they had created together.

Chapter 19

• •

Back to the Future

That was the story of Amanda and Mildred: two young girls who, in their own way, once feared each other, but learned to be the best of friends. Because of their odd way of becoming friends, perfect strangers became family. But what happened to them twenty years later? Where did their life experiences take them?

Well, Mildred and Amanda did remain best friends for a while. Fifteen years into their friendship, Eric was given a better work opportunity in the state of Michigan and the Muses ended up moving there. Despite the distance, the girls kept in touch through social media and technology. It was never the same though. Mildred got married, and Amanda was very focused on her career.

At thirty-three, Amanda was not yet married, but was very successful as a broadcaster in a local radio station and was working toward becoming an anchorwoman for the local news.

Mildred continued her education and eventually became a social worker. She never moved from Lakewood and lived there with her husband, Mike, a fellow she met in college.

Junior had become a barista at a popular coffee shop before leaving Colorado. Mildred had gotten him a job at the same coffee shop she was working in while attending college. She trained him herself and he learned how to prepare coffee rather quickly and well. He was a natural actually. When the family moved to Michigan, he was able to continue working as a barista at another coffee shop in Michigan because it was the only thing he felt comfortable doing.

Even though Vicky and Eric were very proud of all of their children, they were especially proud of Kevin. At the age of twenty-three, he was finishing medical school and was doing his internship as Dr. Kevin Muse in the Dominican Republic where he met his fiancé. There, he was known as 'El Americanito' which is Spanish for 'The Little American.'

Joe ended up dating Mrs. Clancy, Mildred's math teacher, for many years.

After thirteen years of dating, they finally decided to tie the knot. Bo was Joe's best man at their wedding. Mrs. Riley had her own home, so Joe moved to her place.

Eleven years after Bo got Nechi, she wandered off and went missing. Despite endless efforts to find Nechi, Bo never found her. Three years after losing Nechi, James 'Bo' Anderson, died of a massive heart attack. He never married and lived alone all of his life. He had been dead for two days before Joe found him in his apartment. Bo's health had deteriorated due to his past medical issues and poor diet. His life after being rescued by the Muses was a very good life and he never complained about it, not even once. Bo was employed by the same company till his dying day. Everybody was really sad to learn of his death.

As for Lucinda, she went off to Denver and became a very successful attorney.

She got married and had a daughter. Her husband, who was also an attorney, bought her a big, beautiful house. They lived very comfortably and very happily.

Daniel also moved to Denver and became an executive chef at a five-star restaurant. He was happily married and became the father of twin girls. He continued to keep in touch with Lucinda who lived very close to him. His twin girls became friends with Lucinda's daughter and both families often hung out.

Sky moved to Colorado Springs and became a physical therapist. Like Amanda, she was also single, only she was aggressively looking for someone. Liz Lombardi moved to Los Angeles and opened a tanning and spa salon. She never heard from Sharon, Mildred, nor anybody else from Lakewood Junior High again. She never even bothered looking.

When Jennifer was released, she struggled with finding a job. She ended up moving in with Lola, Luke's great-grandmother. Shortly after, Lola became very ill. Jennifer stayed and cared for Lola until Lola passed. Lola left Jennifer her life's savings and her house so that Jennifer may go back to school and be able to provide for Luke.

Jennifer decided to go to beauty school and get her degree. Although she struggled in the beginning, she did eventually open her very own beauty salon right in her home. As soon as the word got out, her business did very well.

Unfortunately, things did not work out so well for Luke. He ended up dropping out of school and was also struggling with drugs and petty crimes. Mildred did everything in her power to help her brother, but eventually, she gave up the fight.

Luke knew that he could always count on his sister whenever he decided to turn his life around.

There you have it: the journeys of these lives and how they got to where they are today. The thing is, they are still not done. With the exception of Bo, they are still 'under construction.' Nobody really knows what God has in store for them or what changes they will undergo. Even Luke, who is not in a good place right now, can turn his life around if he wanted to. He can also make a difference in someone else's life. Who's to say that Luke can't one day make a positive contribution to society? If we base it on his actions today, then maybe not; but what if we treat and see him as someone who can? It worked for Mildred, didn't it? It can work for anyone.